PROOF OF THEIR
ONE-NIGHT
PASSION

PROOF OF THEIR ONE-NIGHT PASSION

LOUISE FULLER

MILLS & BOON

First published in Great Britain 2019
by Mills & Boon, an imprint of HarperCollins*Publishers*
1 London Bridge Street, London, SE1 9GF

Large Print edition 2020

© 2019 Louise Fuller

ISBN: 978-0-263-08435-1

Printed and bound in Great Britain
by CPI Group (UK) Ltd, Croydon, CR0 4YY

To Georgia.
For endlessly listening to my rants
and for sending me cheering photos
of chickens and rabbits.
All my love. X

CHAPTER ONE

RUBBING HER EYES, Lottie Dawson drew the curtain back and gazed out of her bedroom window. The garden was in darkness, but she could hear the steady patter of the rain, and in the glow of the night light the glass was speckled with fat blobs of water.

Yawning, she glanced over at the clock beside her bed.

It was only five-thirty a.m., an unpleasant hour at most times of the year, but particularly so on a cold, wet November day in rural Suffolk. But for once her eleven-month-old daughter's early-morning routine was an advantage. Today they were going to London, and she actually needed to get up.

Turning round, she glanced over to where Sóley was standing in her cot, her blonde curls flattened against her head, her mouth clamped around the edge of her teddy bear.

As Lottie walked towards her she held up her fat little arms and began dancing on the spot.

'Hi.' Leaning forward, she lifted her daughter up, pressing her body close.

Her heart swelled. She was so beautiful, so perfect. Born in December, on the shortest day of the year, she had been as golden and welcome as the unseasonal sun that had come out to celebrate her birth and inadvertently suggested her name.

'Let's go get you some milk,' she murmured, inhaling the clean, sweet smell of her daughter's skin.

Downstairs, she switched the light on in the kitchen and frowned. A frying pan sat in the sink and the remains of a bacon sandwich were congealing on a plate on the crumb-strewn table. Beside it stood an open tool box and a tattoo gun.

Lottie gritted her teeth. She loved living with her brother Lucas, and he was brilliant with Sóley, but he was six foot four, and it sometimes felt that their tiny cottage wasn't big enough for him—especially as his idea of domesticity was taking his boots off to sleep.

Tutting under her breath, she shifted Sóley's weight to her hip. 'Look at all this mess Uncle

Lucas has made,' she said softly, gazing down into her daughter's wide blue eyes.

There was no time to deal with it now. Not if she was going to get herself and Sóley dressed and up to London by eleven o'clock. As she filled the kettle her pulse skipped forward. The gallery in Islington was tiny, but it was hosting her first solo show since giving birth.

Incredibly, some of the pieces had already sold and it was great to know that her work had an audience but, more importantly, the Barker Foundation wanted to talk to her about a commission. Getting funding was a huge step up. Not only would it allow her to continue working without having to teach in the evenings, but she might also be able to extend her workshop.

Glancing into the living room at the dark shape on her sofa, she imagined her brother's eye-rolling reaction to her pragmatism.

Ever since she'd bought the cottage he'd been teasing her about selling out, joking that getting a mortgage was the first step towards the dark side. As far as he and their mother Izzy knew the money had come from a private commission, and Lucas had a very dim view of private clients believing they were only interested in buying art as an investment rather than out of aesthetic appreciation.

She bit her lip. She hated lying to them, but telling the truth—that the deposit for the cottage had been given to her by her biological father, a man who up until two years ago hadn't even known she existed—was just not an option.

Having tested the milk on her tongue, she handed the bottle to Sóley and they both retreated upstairs. Pulling open drawers, she thought back to the moment when she had finally met Alistair Bannon in a motorway service station.

Her stomach clenched. She'd spent so many hours as a child staring into a mirror, trying to work out which of her features came from that man, but even before he had opened his mouth it had been obvious that he was not looking to reconnect with a fully-grown daughter. It wasn't that he didn't accept her as his child—just that he felt no urgency to know her, and their meeting had been strange and strained and short.

From downstairs, she heard the clump of boots hitting the floor. Lucas was up.

She wondered how her brother would react if she showed him the letter her father had sent afterwards. It was polite, carefully worded to offer no obvious rejection but no hope either, basically saying she was a remarkable young woman and he wished her well. Enclosed with the letter had been a cheque for an amount that he hoped would cover his financial contributions for the years he had missed.

Staring at his signature on the cheque, she had felt sick, stunned that she could be reduced to a four-digit sum, and she'd been tempted to tear it up. Only then she'd got pregnant.

Stripping off, she gazed down at her naked body, at the silvery stretch marks that were still faintly visible on her stomach.

Becoming a mother had been so far away in her future plans that she hadn't even suspected she was pregnant but, having been unable to shift a persistent stomach upset she had gone to the doctor, and three days and one urine sample later she had officially been having a baby.

A baby who, like her, was going to grow up never knowing her father. She still wasn't entirely sure how it had happened. They had used protection, but that first time had been so frantic, so urgent, somehow it must have failed.

Shivering, she pulled on her clothes, trying to ignore the sudden thumping of her heart.

She could still remember the night her daughter was conceived. She doubted she would ever forget it. It was like a fever in her blood. The heat and the frenzy had faded, but the memory remained in her bones and on her skin, so that sometimes she'd catch sight of the back of a blond head and a pair of wide shoulders and would have to stop and close her eyes against the urgency of wanting him.

Ragnar Steinn.

She would never forget him either.

It would be impossible.

It would be like trying to forget the sun.

But, despite having the muscular body and clean-cut profile of a Norse god, he had shown himself to be depressingly human in his behaviour. Not only had he lied about where he was staying, and about wanting to spend the day with her, he'd sneaked off before she'd woken up.

And yet together they had made Sóley, and no amount of lies or hardship or loneliness would ever make her regret her beautiful daughter.

'Looks like we've got snow coming,' Lucas said as she walked into the tiny sitting room, holding Sóley on her hip and munching a piece of toast.

He had switched on the ancient television and was wolfing down the remains of his bacon sandwich.

Catching sight of her expression, he grinned sheepishly. 'Sorry about the mess. Look, I'll tidy up, I promise, and I'll chop that wood today. Get it all stacked before the temperatures drop. Do you want me to have little Miss Sunshine?'

She shook her head. 'No, but you could give us a lift to the station.'

'Okay—but only if I get a cuddle.'

He held up his hands and Sóley leaned towards him, grabbing at his shirt collar. Watching her brother's face soften Lottie felt her anger and resentment fade as he pulled the little girl into his arms, wincing as she reached for his hair and grabbed it tightly in her fist.

Unpeeling her fingers, he handed his niece a piece of banana and glanced up at his sister. 'You couldn't put the kettle on as you're up—?'

Glancing at the clock on the wall, Lottie did a quick calculation in her head. There was time before she had to leave. She sighed. 'I'll make some tea.'

Rinsing out the teapot, she put the kettle on the stove.

'You know, I think Sóley is a lot more with it than most kids her age,' she heard Lucas say.

'You do?' Smiling, she poured water into the pot. For someone so laid-back, her brother was extremely partisan and competitive when it came to his niece.

'Yeah—I mean, she's watching the news like she knows what's going on.'

'Good. That means we can outvote you when the football's on.'

'No, seriously, she's completely transfixed by this guy—Lottie, come and look.'

'Okay, I'm coming.'

Walking back into the sitting room, she looked over to where her daughter had pulled herself up in front of the television.

Lucas was right, Sóley did seem to be fascinated. Pulling her gaze away from her daughter's plump cheeks, Lottie glanced at the screen.

The interviewer—a woman—was gazing at the man opposite her with the same fascination as her daughter, so that for a moment Lottie only registered his blond hair and eyes that were the cool, clear blue of a glacier. Then slowly his features came into focus and she felt her mouth slide open.

It was him.

It was Ragnar.

She had wanted to find him after she'd found out she was pregnant, and then again when their daughter was born. But both of them had shut down their profiles on the dating app they'd used to meet up, and there had been no trace of any Ragnar Steinn—or at least none that looked like him—on any internet search.

Her jaw tensed. Not that it would have changed anything if she had managed to get in touch. His clumsy lies had made it clear enough that he'd only been interested in her for one night only, so he was hardly going to jump at the news that he'd fathered a child with her.

She watched mutely, ice working its way up her spine, as Sóley began patting the screen. Her heart was jumping in her chest.

'Who is he?' she asked. 'I mean, why is he on TV?'

She had been aiming for offhand, but her voice sounded thin and breathless.

Thankfully, though, Lucas was too distracted to notice.

'Ragnar Stone. He owns that dating app. Apparently he's launching a VIP version.'

'Dating app?' she said woodenly. It felt as if she had stopped breathing.

She was about to ask which one, but there was no point. She already knew the answer. Only she'd thought he was like her—someone using the app to meet people. She hadn't known that he owned it—in fact, thinking about it, she was certain that he hadn't mentioned that to her.

'You know—*ice/breakr*?'

Lucas glanced up at her, and she watched his face still as his brain caught up with his mouth.

'Course you do...' he said quietly.

It had been Lucas who had signed her up to the app. Lucas who had coaxed her into replying to the 'ice breaker' question. It could be on any topic from politics to holidays. Not all of the questions were profound, but they were designed to spark an instinctive response that apparently helped match couples more accurately than a photo and a list of likes and dislikes. She knew he felt responsible for everything that had happened, but she was too stunned and angry to dismiss his obvious guilt.

Ragnar *Stone*!

So he'd even lied about his name.

And he hadn't just been using the app—*he owned it*.

She breathed out unsteadily, trying to absorb this new version of the facts as she'd known them, grateful that her brother's attention was still fixed on the TV and not on her face. Grateful, too, that she hadn't shown him Ragnar's profile at the time.

Her skin was trembling.

'Is he in London?' she asked.

'Yeah, for the launch. He's got an office here.' Lucas wiped Sóley's mouth with the hem of his shirt and met her gaze. 'One of those converted warehouses in Docklands. You know Nick?'

She nodded. Nick was one of Lucas's cohorts. He played drums in their band, but in his day job he was a graffiti artist.

'He did this huge old-school design the whole length of Ragnar Stone's building. He showed me some pictures and it looks really sick.' He nodded his head approvingly.

Lottie cleared her throat. 'Did he meet him?'

Lucas frowned. 'Nah. Best you can hope with a guy like Stone is that you catch a ride on his slipstream.'

She blinked. Yes, she supposed it was. That was basically what had happened twenty months ago in her hotel room. If she hadn't understood that before, her brother's words made it clear now that she and Sóley were not permanent features of that ride.

'So what time do you want me to drop you off?'

Taking a shallow breath, she looked over at her brother, but her eyes never reached his face. Instead she felt her gaze stretch past him to the TV screen, like a compass point seeking the magnetic north. She stared at Ragnar's face, the artist in her responding to the clean symmetry of his features and the woman in her remembering the pressure of his mouth. He was so beautiful, and so very like his blonde, blue-eyed daughter in every way—except the dimples in her cheeks, which were entirely her own.

She felt something twist inside her. What if it was more than just looks? Growing up not knowing where half her DNA came from had been hard when her mother and brother were so alike in character. It had made her feel incomplete and unfinished, and even finally meeting her father hadn't changed that. It had been too late for them to form a bond and get to know one another.

But would it have been different if he'd found out about her when she was a baby? And, more importantly, could she consciously deny her own child the chance of having what she had so desperately wanted for herself?

The seconds ticked by as she wondered what to do. He would have a PA for sure—only she couldn't tell them why she was ringing. But would they put her through to him without a reason? She bit her lip. More importantly, could she honestly go through with it? Tell him over the phone that he was a father?

She cleared her throat. 'Actually, Lucas, could you have Sóley for me after all?' she said, glancing over at her daughter. 'There's something I need to do. In person.'

Being interviewed was probably his least favourite part of being a CEO, Ragnar Stone decided, as he stood up and shook hands with the earnest-faced young man in front of him. It was so repetitive, and most of the answers could easily have been given by even the most junior member of his PR department. But, as his head of media Madeline Thomas had told him that morning, people were 'in thrall to the personality behind the brand', so he had dutifully worked his way through twenty-two interviews with just a half-hour break for lunch.

And now he was done.

Shrugging off his jacket, he loosened his tie and pulled a black hoodie over his head as his PA Adam came into the room.

'What time is the car coming to pick me up in the morning?' he asked, reaching down to pick up a slim laptop from his desk.

'Six-thirty. You have a meeting with James Milner at seven, you're seeing the graphics team at eight, and then breakfast with Caroline Woodward.'

'I'll see you tomorrow.' Ragnar smiled briefly at his PA. 'And thanks for keeping it moving today, Adam.'

Stepping into the lift, he ran his hand over his face. Only one more week and then, once this final round of publicity was over and the new app went live, he was going to take some time away from all this.

He knew he'd left it too long. His annual two-week recharge ritual had dwindled to a couple of snatched days, but since launching *ice/breakr* two years ago life had been insane.

Working long hours, eating and sleeping on the move in a series of hotel rooms, and of course in the background his gorgeous, crazy, messy family, acting out their own modern-day Norse saga of betrayal and blackmail.

Glancing down at his phone, he grimaced. Three missed calls from his half-sister Marta, four from his mother, six texts from his stepmother Anna, and twelve from his stepbrother Gunnar.

Stretching his neck and shoulders, he slipped

his phone into the pocket of his hoodie. None of it would be urgent. It never was. But, like all drama queens, his family loved an audience.

For once they could wait. Right now he wanted to hit the gym and then crash out.

The lift doors opened and he flipped his hood up over his head, nodding at the receptionists as he walked past their desk and out into the dark night air.

He didn't hear their polite murmurs of good-night, but he heard the woman's voice so clearly that it seemed to come from inside his head.

'Ragnar.'

In the moment that followed he realised two things. One, he recognised the voice, and two, his heart was beating hard and fast like a hail-storm against his ribs.

As he turned he got an impression of slight-ness, coupled with tension, and then his eyes focused on the woman standing in front of him.

Her light brown hair was longer, her pale face more wary, but she looked just as she had twenty-odd months ago. And yet she seemed different in a way he couldn't pin down. Younger, maybe? Or perhaps she just looked younger because most of the women in his circles routinely wore make-up, whereas she was bare-faced.

'I was just passing. I've got an exhibition up the road...' She waved vaguely towards the window. 'I saw you coming out.' She hesitated. 'I don't know if you remember me...?'

'I remember.'

He cut across her, but only because hearing her voice was messing with his head. It was a voice he had never forgotten—a voice that had called out his name under very different circumstances in a hotel room less than a mile away from where they were standing.

He watched her pupils dilate, and knew that she was thinking the same thing.

For a second they stared at one another, the memory of the night they shared quivering between them, and then, leaning forward, he gave her a quick, neutral hug.

Or it was meant to be neutral, but as his cheek brushed against hers the warm, floral scent of her skin made his whole body hum like a power cable.

Stepping back, he gave her a small, taut smile and something pulsed between them, a flicker of corresponding heat that made his skin grow tight.

'Of course I remember. It's Lottie—Lottie Dawson.'

'Yes, that's *my* name.'

Seeing the accusation in her eyes, he felt his chest tighten, remembering the lies he'd told her. It wasn't hard to remember. Growing up in the truth-shifting environment of his family had left him averse to lying, but that night had been an exception—a necessary and understandable exception. He'd met her through a dating app, but as the app's creator and owner, anonymity had seemed like a sensible precaution.

But his lies hadn't all been about concealing his identity. His family's chaotic and theatrical affairs had left him wary of even the hint of a relationship, so when he'd woken to find himself planning the day ahead with Lottie he'd got up quietly and left—because planning a day with a woman was not on his agenda.

Ever.

His life was already complicated enough. He had parents and step-parents, and seven whole and half-and step siblings scattered around the world, and not one of them had made a relationship last for any length of time. Not only that, their frequent and overlapping affairs and break-ups, and the inevitable pain and misery they caused, seemed to be an unavoidable accompaniment to any kind of commitment.

He liked life to be straightforward. Simple. Honest. It was why he'd created *ice/breakr* in the first place. Why make dating so needlessly confusing? When by asking and answering one carefully curated question people could match their expectations and so avoid any unnecessary emotional trauma.

Or that was the theory.

Only clearly there been some kind of glitch— a ghost in the machine, maybe?

'So it's not Steinn, then?'

His eyes met hers. She was not classically beautiful, but she was intriguing. Both ordinary and extraordinary at once. Mousy hair, light brown eyes… And yet her face had a capacity for expression that was mesmerising.

And then there was her voice.

It wasn't just the huskiness that made his skin tingle, but the way she lingered over the syllables of certain words, like a blues singer. Had he judged her simply on her voice, he might have assumed she had a lifestyle to match—too many late nights and a history of heartache, but their night together had revealed a lack of confidence and a clumsiness that suggested the opposite. Not that he'd asked or minded. In fact it had only made her feverish response to him even more arousing.

Feeling his body respond to the memory of her flowering desire, he blocked his thoughts and shrugged. 'In a way it is. Steinn is Icelandic for Stone. It was just a play on words.'

Her eyes held his. 'Oh, you mean like calling your dating app *ice/breakr*?'

So she knew about the app. 'I wanted to try it out for myself. A dummy run, if you like.'

She flinched and he felt his shoulders tense.

'I didn't intend to deceive you.'

'About that? Or about wanting to spend the day with me?' She frowned. 'Wouldn't it have been fairer and more honest if you'd just said you didn't want to spend any more time with me?'

Ragnar stared at her in silence, gritting his teeth against the sting of her words. Yes, it would. But that would have been a different kind of lie.

Lying didn't come naturally to him—his whole family played fast and loose with the facts and even as a child he'd found it exhausting and stressful. But that night he'd acted out of character, starting from the moment he'd played games with his American father's name and booked a table as Mr Steinn.

And then, the morning after, confronted by his

body's fierce reaction to hers, and that uncharacteristic and unsettling need he'd felt to prolong their time together, the lies had kept coming.

'I didn't—'

'It doesn't matter.' She swiped his answer away with a swift jerk of her hand. 'That's not why I'm here.' She glanced past him into the street. 'There's a café open down the road…'

He knew it. It was one of those brightly lit artisan coffee shops with bearded baristas and clean wooden counters. Nothing like the shadowy, discreet bar where they'd met before.

His heartbeat stalled. He could still remember her walking in. It had been one of those sharply cold March evenings that reminded him of home, and there had been a crush of people at the bar, escaping the wind's chill.

He'd been on the verge of leaving.

A combination of work and family histrionics had shrunk his private life to early-morning sessions with his trainer and the occasional dinner with an investor when, finally, it had dawned on him that his app had been launched for nearly three months.

On a whim, he'd decided to try it out.

But, watching the couples dotted about the

bar, he had felt a familiar unease clutch at his stomach.

Out of habit, he'd got there early. It was a discipline he embraced—perhaps because since childhood any chance to assemble his thoughts in peace had always been such a rarity. But when Lottie had walked through the door rational thought had been swept away. Her cheeks had been flushed, and she'd appeared to be wearing nothing but a pair of slim-heeled boots and a short black trench coat.

Sadly she'd been clothed underneath but he'd stayed sitting down. If using his own dating app had been impulsive, then not leaving by another door had been the first time he'd done something so utterly unconsidered.

'And you want me to join you there?'

Her eyes met his and there was a beat of silence before she nodded.

His pulse accelerated.

It was nearly two years since that night.

He was exhausted.

His head of security would be appalled.

And yet—

His eyes rested on the soft cushion of her mouth.

* * *

The coffee shop was still busy enough that they had to queue for their drinks, but they managed to find a table.

'Thank you.' He gestured towards his *espresso*.

His wallet had been in his hand, but she had sidestepped neatly in front of him, her soft brown eyes defying him to argue with her. Now, though, those same brown eyes were busily avoiding his, and for the first time since she'd called out his name he wondered why she had tracked him down.

He drank his coffee, relishing the heat and the way the caffeine started to block the tension in his back.

'So, I'm all yours,' he said quietly.

She stiffened. 'Hardly.'

He sighed. 'Is that what this is about? Me giving you the wrong name.'

Her eyes narrowed. 'No, of course not. I'm not—' She stopped, frowning. 'Actually, I wasn't just passing, and I'm not here for myself.' She took a breath. 'I'm here for Sóley.'

Her face softened into a smile and he felt a sudden urge to reach out and caress the curve of her lip, to trigger such a smile for himself.

'It's a pretty name.'

She nodded, her smile freezing.

It *was* a pretty name—one he'd always liked. One you didn't hear much outside of Iceland. Only what had it got to do with him?

Watching her fingers tremble against her cup, he felt his ribs tighten. 'Who's Sóley?'

She was quiet for less than a minute, only it felt much longer—long enough for his brain to click through all the possible answers to the impossible one.

He watched her posture change from defensive to resolute.

'She's your daughter. Our daughter.'

He stared at her in silence, but a cacophony of questions was ricocheting inside his head.

Not the how or the when or the where, but the *why*. Of course he'd used condoms but that first time he'd been rushing. And he'd known that. So why hadn't he checked everything was okay? Why had he allowed the heat of their encounter to blot out common sense?

But the answers to those questions would have to wait.

'Okay…'

Shifting in her seat, she frowned. '"Okay"?' she repeated. 'Do you understand what I just said?'

'Yes.' He nodded. 'You're saying I got you pregnant.'

'You don't seem surprised,' she said slowly.

He shrugged. 'These things happen.'

To his siblings and half-siblings, even to his mother. But not to him. Never to him.

Until now.

'And you believe me?' She seemed confused, surprised?

Tilting his head, he held her gaze. 'Honest answer?'

He was going to ask her what she would gain by lying. But before he could open his mouth her lip curled.

'On past performance I'm not sure I can expect that. I mean, you lied about your name. And the hotel you were staying at. And you lied about wanting to spend the day with me.'

'I didn't plan on lying to you,' he said quietly.

Her mouth thinned. 'No, I'm sure it comes very naturally to you.'

'You're twisting my words.'

She shook her head. 'You mean like saying Steinn instead of Stone?'

Pressing his spine into the wall behind him, he felt a tick of anger begin to pulse beneath his skin.

'Okay, I was wrong to lie to you—but if you care about the truth so much then why have you waited so long to tell me that I have a daughter? I mean, she must be what…?' He did a quick mental calculation. 'Ten, eleven months?'

'Eleven months,' she said stiffly. 'And I did want to tell you. I tried looking for you when I was pregnant, and then again when she was born. But the only Ragnar Steinns I could track down weren't you.' She shifted in her seat again. 'I probably would never have found you if you hadn't been on the TV.'

He looked at her again, and despite the rush of righteousness heating his blood he could see that she was nervous, could hear the undertone of strain beneath her bravado.

But then it was a hell of a thing to do. To face a man and tell him he had a child.

His heart began to beat faster.

Years spent navigating through the maelstrom of his family's dramas had given him a cast-iron control over his feelings, and yet for some reason he couldn't stop her panic and defiance from getting under his skin.

But letting feelings get in the way of the facts was not going to help the situation. Nor was it going to be much use to his eleventh-month-old daughter.

Right now he needed to focus on the practical.

'Fortunately you did find me,' he said calmly.

'Here.' She was pushing something across the table towards him, but he carried on talking.

'So I'm guessing you want to talk money?'

At that moment a group of young men and women came into the café and began noisily choosing what to drink. As the noise swelled around them Lottie thought she might have misheard.

Only she knew that she hadn't.

Ever since arriving in London that morning she'd been questioning whether she was doing the right thing, and the thought of seeing Ragnar again had made her stomach perform an increasingly complicated gymnastics routine. Her mood had kept alternating between angry and nervous, but when he'd walked out into the street her mood had been forgotten and a spasm of almost unbearable hunger had consumed everything.

If she'd thought seeing him on TV had prepared her for meeting him again then she'd been wrong. Beneath the street lighting his beauty had been as stark and shocking as the volcanic rock of his homeland.

And he was almost unbearably like the daughter they shared. Only now it would appear that, just like her own father, Ragnar seemed to have already decided the terms of his relationship.

'Money?' She breathed out unsteadily. The word tasted bitter in her mouth. 'I didn't come here to talk to you about money. I came here to talk about our daughter.'

Her heart felt suddenly too big for her chest. Why did this keep happening? Why did men think that they could reduce her life to some random sum of money?

'Children cost money.' He held her gaze. 'Clearly you've been supporting her alone up until now and I want to fix that. I'll need to talk to my lawyers, but I want you to know that you don't need to worry about that anymore.'

I'm not worrying, she wanted to scream at him. She wasn't asking to be helped financially, or fixed. In fact she wasn't asking for anything at all.

'I've not been alone. My mother helps, and my brother Lucas lives with me. He works as a tattooist so he can choose his own hours—'

'A tattooist?'

Glancing up, she found his clear blue eyes examining her dispassionately, as if she was some flawed algorithm. She felt slightly sick—just as she had in those early months of the pregnancy. Only that had been a welcome sickness. A proof of new life, a sign of a strong pregnancy. Now, though, the sickness was down to the disconnect between the man who had reached for her so frantically in that hotel room and this cool-eyed stranger.

She stared at him in silence.

What made this strange, unnerving distance between them a hundred times harder was that she had let herself be distracted by his resemblance to Sóley. Let herself hope that the connection between Ragnar and his daughter would be more than it had been for her and her own father—not just bones and blood, but a willingness to claim her as his own.

But the cool, dispassionate way he had turned the conversation immediately to money was proof that he'd reached the limit of his parental involvement.

She cleared her throat. 'I know you're a rich man, Ragnar, but I didn't come here to beg.' She swallowed down her regret and disappointment. 'This was a mistake. Don't worry, though, it's not one I'll make again—so why don't you get back to the thing that clearly matters most to you? Making money.'

Ragnar reached across the table, but even before he'd got to his feet she had scraped back her seat and snatched up her coat, and he watched in disbelief as she turned and fled from the cafe.

For a moment he considered chasing after her, but she was moving fast and no doubt would already have reached the underground station on the corner.

He sat back down; his chest tight with an all too familiar frustration.

Her behaviour—having a child with a complete stranger, keeping that child a secret, turning up unannounced to reveal the child's existence and then storming off—could have come straight from his family's playbook of chaos.

Glancing down, he felt his pulse scamper forward as for the first time he looked at what she'd pushed across the table. It was a photo of a little girl.

A little girl who looked exactly like him—Sóley.

Reaching out, he touched her face lightly. She was so small, so golden, just like her name. And he was not going to let her grow up with no influence but her chaotic mother and whatever ragtag family she had in tow.

He might love his own family, but he knew only too well the downside of growing up in the eye of a storm and he didn't want that for his daughter.

So arrangements would have to be made.

Picking up the photo, he slid it into his wallet and pulled out his phone.

CHAPTER TWO

HITCHING HER SLEEPING daughter further up on to her shoulder, Lottie glanced around the gallery.

Groups of people were moving slowly around the room, occasionally pausing to gaze more closely at the sketches and collages and sculpted resin objects before moving on again. It wasn't rammed, but she was pleased—she really was. She was also exhausted.

'Nearly over.'

She turned, eyes widening, and then began to smile as the woman standing beside her gave her a conspiratorial wink. Slim, blonde, and with the kind of cheekbones that grazed men's eyes as they walked past, Georgina Hamilton was the gallery's glamorous and incredibly competent co-owner, and despite the fact that she and Lottie were different in as many ways as it was possible to be, she had become an ally and fierce supporter.

Lottie screwed up her face. 'Do I look that desperate?'

Her friend stared at her critically. 'Only to me. To everyone else you probably just look artistically dishevelled.' She glanced at the sleeping Sóley. 'Do you want me to take her?'

Their eyes met and then they both began to giggle. They both knew that Georgina's idea of hands-on childcare was choosing baby clothes in her cousin's upmarket Chelsea boutique.

'No, it's okay. I don't want to risk waking her.' Lottie looked down at the top of her daughter's soft, golden-haired head. 'She's been really unsettled the last couple of nights.'

And she wasn't the only one.

Her cheeks were suddenly warm, and she tilted her head away from Georgina's gaze. It was true that Sóley was struggling to fall asleep at night, but it was Ragnar who had actually been keeping her awake.

It wasn't just the shock of seeing him again, or even his disappointingly predictable reduction of their daughter's life to a financial settlement. It was the disconcerting formality between them.

She pressed her face into her daughter's hair. The disconnect between her overtly erotic memories of the last time they'd met and his cool reserve in the coffee shop had made her feel as if she'd stepped through the looking glass. He had been at once so familiar, and yet so different. Gone was the passion and the febrile hunger, and in their place was a kind of measured, almost clinical gaze that had made her feel she was being judged—and found wanting.

Her heartbeat twitched. And yet running alongside their laboured conversation there had been something pulsing beneath the surface—a stirring of desire, something intimate yet intangible that had made her fingers clumsy as she'd tried to pick up her cup.

She blinked the thought away. Of course what had happened between them had clearly been a blip. After all, this was a man who had turned people's need for intimacy into a global business worth billions—an ambition that was hardly compatible with empathy or passion.

Her jaw tightened. What was it he'd said about that night? Oh, yes, that it had been a 'dummy run' for his app. Well, *she* was a dummy for thinking he might have actually wanted to get to know his daughter.

From now on she was done with doing the right thing for the wrong people. She was only going to let the people she could trust get close—like the woman standing in front of her.

'Thanks for staying, Georgina, and for everything you've done. I honestly don't think I would have sold as well if you hadn't been here.'

Swinging her cape of gleaming blonde hair over her shoulder, Georgina smiled back at her. 'Oh, sweetie, you don't need to thank me—firstly, it's my job, and secondly it's much better for the gallery to have a sold-out exhibition.'

'Sold out?' She blinked in confusion. 'But I thought there were still three pieces left—those sketches and the collage—?'

Georgina shrugged. 'Not any more. Rowley's contacted me at lunchtime and bought all of them.'

Lottie felt her ribs tighten. Rowley's was a prestigious art dealer with a Mayfair address and a client list of wealthy investors who flitted between Beijing, New York, and London, spending millions on houses and cars and emerging artists.

They also had an unrivalled reputation for discretion.

She opened her mouth, but Georgina was already shaking her head.

'No, they didn't give me a name.' She raised an eyebrow. 'You don't look very pleased.'

'I am,' Lottie protested.

After finding out she was pregnant, working had been a welcome distraction from the upheaval in her life, but it had quickly become much more.

She glanced at the visitors who were still drifting around the gallery. 'I just prefer to meet the buyers directly.'

'I know you do—but you know what these collectors are like. They love to have the cachet of buying up-and-coming artists' early work, but they love their anonymity more.' Georgina tutted. 'I know you hate labels, but you are up-and-coming. If you don't believe me then believe your own eyes. You can see all the "Sold" stickers from here.' Watching Lottie shift her daughter's weight to her other arm, she said, 'Are you sure I can't take her?'

Lottie shook her head. 'It's fine. They must be on their way. I mean, Lucas was supposed to meet Izzy at the station and then they were coming straight back.'

Georgina sniffed. She was not a huge fan of Lottie's family. 'Yes, well... I expect they got "distracted".' She smoothed the front of her sculpted nip and tuck dress, and then her eyes narrowed like a tigress spotting her prey. 'Oh, my…' she said softly.

'What's the matter?' Lottie frowned.

'Don't look now but an incredibly hot guy has just walked into the gallery. He has the most amazing eyes I've ever seen.''

Lottie shook her head. No doubt they were fixed on the woman standing beside her.

'Ouch.' She winced as Georgina clutched at her arm.

'He's coming over to us.'

'To you, you mean—and of course he is,' Lottie said drily. 'He's male.'

Georgina had the most incredible effect on men, and she was used to simply filling the space beside her.

'He's not looking at me,' Georgina said slowly. She sounded stunned. 'He's looking at *you.*'

Lottie laughed. 'Perhaps he hasn't put his contact lenses in this morning. Or maybe he—'

She turned and her words stopped mid-sentence. Her body seemed to turn to salt. Walking towards her, his blue eyes pinning her to the floor, was Ragnar Stone.

She stared at him mutely as he stopped in front of her. He was dressed more casually than when she'd stopped him outside his office, but such was the force of his presence that suddenly the gallery seemed much smaller and there was a shift in tension, as though everyone was looking at him while trying to appear as though they weren't.

His blue eyes really were incredibly blue, she thought weakly. But Georgina had been wrong. He wasn't looking at her. Instead, his eyes were fixed on his daughter. For a few half-seconds, maybe more, he gazed at Sóley, his face expressionless and unmoving, and then slowly he turned his head towards her.

'Hello, Lottie.'

She stared at him silence, her heartbeat filling her chest, her grip tightening around her daughter's body. In the café there had been so much noise, but here in the near museum-level quiet of the gallery his voice was making her body quiver like a violin being tuned.

It was completely illogical and inappropriate, but that didn't stop it being true.

'Hello, Ragnar,' she said stiffly. 'I wasn't expecting to see you.'

She wasn't sure what kind of a response he would make to her remark, but maybe he felt the same way because he didn't reply.

'So you two know one another, then?' Georgina said brightly.

'Yes.'

'No!'

They both spoke as one—him quietly, her more loudly.

Lottie felt her cheeks grow warm. 'We met once a couple of years back,' she said quickly.

'Just shy of two years.'

Ragnar's blue eyes felt like lasers.

There was a short, strained silence and then Georgina cleared her throat. 'Well, I'll let you catch up on old times.'

Clearly dazzled by Ragnar's beauty, she smiled at him sweetly and, blind to Lottie's pleading expression, sashayed towards an immaculately dressed couple on the other side of the room.

'How did you find me?' she said stiffly. Her heart bumped unsteadily against her ribs. She was still processing the fact that he had come here.

He held her gaze. 'Oh, I was just passing.'

Remembering the lie she'd told, she glared at him. 'Did you have me followed?'

Something flickered across the blue of his pupils. 'Not followed, no—but I did ask my head of security to locate the exhibition you mentioned.'

A pulse was beating in her head. His being here was just so unexpected. Almost as unexpected as the feeling of happiness that was fluttering in time to her heart.

'Aren't you going to introduce me?'

For a moment she gazed at Ragnar in confusion. Was he talking about Georgina? A mixture of disbelief and jealousy twisted her breathing. Was he really using this moment to hit on another woman?

'Her name's Georgina. She's—'

'Not her.'

She heard the tension in his voice before she noticed it in the rigidity of his jaw.

'My daughter.'

Her heart shrank inside her ribs.

In the twenty-four hours since she'd left Ragnar, and his unsolicited offer of financial help, she'd tried hard to arrange her emotions into some kind of order. They hadn't responded. Instead she had kept struggling with the same anger and disappointment she'd felt after meeting her father. But at least she had been able to understand if not excuse Alistair's reluctance to get involved. Meeting an adult daughter he hadn't even known existed was never going to be easy, but Sóley wasn't even one yet.

Okay, at first maybe she would have been a little cautious around him—although remembering her daughter's transfixed gaze when Ragnar had come on the television screen maybe not. But even if she had been understandably hesitant it would have passed, and he could have become a father to her.

Only he'd immediately turned their relationship into a balance sheet. Or that was what she'd thought he'd done. But if that was the case then what was he doing here, asking to be introduced to his daughter?

There was only one way to find out. She cleared her throat. 'What do you want, Ragnar?'

'Exactly what I wanted yesterday evening,' he said softly. 'Only instead of giving me the chance to explain you used the moment to have some kind of temper tantrum.'

She stared at him, a pulse of anger hopping over her skin. 'I did give you a chance and you offered me money,' she snapped. 'And if that's why you're here then you've wasted your time. I told you I didn't want your money and nothing's changed.'

'That's not your choice to make.' He held her gaze. 'I mean, what kind of mother turns down financial help for her child?'

She felt her cheeks grow hot. He was twisting her words. That wasn't what had happened. Or maybe it was, but it hadn't been about her turning down his money as much as proving him wrong about her motive for getting in touch.

'I wasn't turning down your money—just your assumption that it was what I wanted,' she said carefully. 'You made me feel cheap.'

His face didn't change. 'So what did you want from me?'

His question caught her off-guard. Not because she didn't know the answer—she did. Partly she had wanted to do the right thing, but also she knew what it had felt like to grow up without any knowledge of her father, and she had wanted to spare her daughter that sense of always feeling on the outside, looking in.

Only it felt odd admitting something so personal to a man who was basically a stranger.

'You're her father. I wanted you to know that,' she said finally. 'I wanted you to know her.' Her voice shook a little as she glanced down at her still sleeping daughter. 'She's so happy and loving, and so interested in everything going on around her.'

'Is that why you brought her to the gallery?'

She frowned, the tension in her stomach nipping tighter. 'Yes, it is,' she said defensively.

He might simply have been making polite conversation, but there was an undercurrent in his voice that reminded her of the moment when she'd told him that Lucas was a tattooist. But how could a man like Ragnar understand her loving but unconventional family? He had made a career of turning the spontaneity of human chemistry into a flow chart.

'I'm an artist *and* a mother. I'm not going to pretend that my daughter isn't a part of my life, nor do I see why I should have to.'

His eyes flickered—or maybe it was the light changing as a bus momentarily passed in front of the gallery's windows.

'I agree,' he said, his gaze shifting from his daughter's sleeping face to one of Lottie's opaque, resin sculptures. 'Being a mother doesn't define you. But it brings new contours to your work. Not literally.' He gave her a small, tight smile. 'But in how it's shaping who you are as an artist.'

Lottie felt her heart press against her ribs. The first time they had met they hadn't really discussed their careers. It felt strange to admit it, given what had happened later in the evening but they hadn't talked about anything personal, and yet it had felt as though their conversation had flowed.

Perhaps she had just been carried along by the energy in the bar, or more likely it had been the rush of adrenalin at having finally gone on a date through the app Lucas had found.

She'd had boyfriends—nothing serious or long-lasting, just the usual short-term infatuation followed by disbelief that she had ever found the object of her affections in any way attractive. But after her meeting with Alistair she had felt crushed, rejected.

Unlovable.

Perhaps if she'd been able to talk to her mother or brother about her feelings it would have been easier, but she'd already felt disloyal, going behind their backs. And why upset them when it had all been for nothing?

Her biological father's panicky need to get back to his life had made her feel ashamed of who she was, and that feeling of not being good enough to deserve his love had coloured her confidence with men generally.

Until Ragnar.

Her pulse twitched. Her nerves had been jangling like a car alarm when she'd walked into the bar. But when Ragnar had stood up in front of her, with his long dark coat curling around his ankles like a cape, her nerves had been swept away not just by his beauty, but his composure. The noisy, shifting mass of people had seemed to fall back so that it was just the two of them in a silence that had felt like a held breath.

She had never felt such a connection with anyone—certainly not with any man. For her—and she'd thought for him too—that night had been an acknowledgement of that feeling and she'd never wanted it to end. In the wordless oblivion of their passion he had made her feel strong and desirable.

Now, though, he felt like a stranger, and she could hardly believe that they had created a child together.

Her ribs squeezed tightly as Sóley wriggled against her and then went limp as she plugged her thumb into her mouth.

'So why are you here?' she said quietly.

'I want to be a part of my daughter's life—and, yes that includes contributing financially, but more importantly I want to have a hands-on involvement in co-parenting her.'

Co-parenting.

The word ricocheted inside her head.

Her throat seemed to have shrunk, so that suddenly it was difficult to breathe, and her heart was leaping erratically like a fish on a hook.

But why? He was offering her exactly what she'd thought she wanted for her daughter, wasn't he?

She felt Sóley move against her again, and instantly her panic increased tenfold.

The truth was that she hadn't really thought about anything beyond Ragnar's initial reaction to finding out he was a father. The memory of her own father's glazed expression of shock and panic had still been uppermost in her mind when she'd found out she was pregnant, and that was what she'd wanted to avoid by getting in touch with Ragnar while their daughter was still tiny.

But had she thought beyond the moment of revelation? Had she imagined him being a hands-on presence in Sóley's life? No, not really. She'd been so self-righteous about Ragnar's deceit, but now it turned out that she had been deceiving herself the whole time—telling herself that she'd got in touch because she wanted him in her daughter's life when really it had been as much about rewriting that uncomfortable, unsatisfactory scene between herself and Alistair.

And now, thanks to her stupidity and shortsightedness, she'd let someone into her life she barely knew or liked who had an agenda that was unlikely to be compatible with hers.

'I don't know how we could make that work—' she began.

But Ragnar wasn't listening. He was staring as though mesmerised at his daughter's face. And, with shock, she realised that Sóley was awake and was staring back at her father. Her heart contracted. Their blue eyes were so alike.

'Hey,' he said softly to his daughter. 'May I?'

His eyes flickered briefly to hers and without realising that she was even doing so she nodded slowly, holding her breath as he held out his hand to Sóley.

Watching her tiny hand clasp his thumb, she felt the same pride and panic she'd felt back in the cottage, when her daughter had been transfixed by Ragnar's face. Whatever *she* felt for him they were father and daughter, and their bond was unassailable.

His next words made it clear that his thoughts were following the same path.

'We need to sit down and talk about what happens next.'

'What happens next…?' she repeated slowly.

He nodded. 'Obviously we'll need to sort out

something legal, but right now I'd like us to be on the same page.'

From somewhere outside in the street a swell of uncontrollable laughter burst into the near-silent gallery. As everyone turned she glanced past Ragnar, feeling the hairs on the back of her neck stand to attention as she spotted the hem of her mother's coat and her brother's familiar black boots stomping down the steps of the gallery.

Panic edged into her head, pushing past all other thought. This wasn't the right time or place for Ragnar to meet her family. She wasn't ready, and nor could she imagine their various reactions to one another. Actually, she could—and it was something she wanted to avoid at all costs.

Her mother would walk a tightrope between charm and contempt. Lucas would probably say something he would regret later.

'Fine,' she said quickly. 'I'll give you my number and you can call me. We can arrange to meet up.'

'I think it would be better if we made a decision now.'

Watching Lucas turning to flirt with the gallery receptionist, Lottie felt her jaw tighten with resentment. Ragnar was pushing her into a corner. Only what choice did she have?

She glanced despairingly as the inner door to the gallery opened. She couldn't risk them meeting one another now, but clearly Ragnar wasn't leaving without a date in place.

'Okay, then—how about tomorrow? After lunch.'

He nodded. 'Would you prefer me to come to you?'

'No—' She practically shouted the word at him. 'People are always dropping in. It'll be easier to talk without any distractions.'

'Fine. I'll send a car.'

'That won't be—'

'Necessary? Perhaps not.' Frowning, he reached into his jacket and pulled out a card. 'But indulge me. This is my private number. Text me your address and I'll have my driver collect you.'

There was a pulse of silence. She disliked the feeling of being treated like some kind of special delivery parcel, but no doubt this was just how his life worked, and refusing seemed childish given what was really at stake.

'Fine—but right now I need you to go. The exhibition will be closing in ten minutes and I want to get Sóley home,' she said, watching with relief as Georgina sped across the gallery to intercept her mother and her brother. 'So if you don't mind—?'

His gaze shifted to her face. 'Of course.' He gave her a smile that barely curved his mouth. 'I'll see you tomorrow.'

Gently he released his grip from Sóley's hand. For a moment he hesitated, his eyes locking with his daughter's, and then he turned and strode towards the door. She watched, her heart in her mouth, as he skirted past her mother and Lucas.

'Sorry we're late!' Her mother ran her hand theatrically through her long dark hair. 'We bumped into Chris and your brother insisted on buying him a drink—'

'I felt awkward.' Lucas shook his head. 'The poor guy practically lost his mind when you dumped him.'

'But never mind about *him.*'

Lottie winced as her mother grabbed her and kissed her on the cheek.

'Who was *that*?' Pivoting round, Izzy gazed after Ragnar with narrowing eyes.

Lottie shrugged. 'He was just passing,' she said quickly.

Lucas frowned. 'I feel like I've seen him before…'

'Unlikely,' Lottie said crisply. 'I don't think

you move in the same circles—and don't try and distract me.' She raised an eyebrow accusingly. 'You were supposed to be here an hour ago. But now that you are here, do you think you could take Sóley for me?'

She watched with relief as Lucas reached out and scooped Sóley into his arms. It wasn't quite as terrifying as the thought of Ragnar meeting her family, but her brother making any kind of connection was something she didn't need. He might just put two and two together and come up with four—and then she would have to lie to his face or, worse, admit the truth to their mother.

There was no way she was getting into all that in public. She'd already over-complicated everything enough by letting a cool-eyed stranger into her life.

But if Ragnar thought her hasty acquiescence to his demands meant that he could set the boundaries for his relationship with their daughter he was wrong—as he was going to find out tomorrow.

Were they her family?

Mounting the steps from the gallery two at a time, Ragnar felt the onset of a familiar unease—that same feeling of being sucked towards a vortex that usually went hand in hand with spending time with his own family.

The scruffy-looking man with Day-of-the-Dead skulls tattooed on his neck and the dark-haired woman wearing an eye-catching red faux-fur coat must be Lottie's brother and mother—and the thought was not exactly reassuring. He knew from dealing with his own family that eccentricities might appear charming to an outsider but usually they went hand in hand with a tendency for self-indulgence and melodrama that was exhausting and time-consuming.

But at least with one's own family you knew what to expect.

Remembering his daughter's hand gripping his thumb, he felt his jaw tighten. Had he been in any way uncertain as to whether he had a role to play in Sóley's life that doubt had instantly and completely vanished as her hand gripped his. Children needed stability and support from the adults in their lives, not drama, and it wasn't hard to imagine exactly what kind of circus those two could create.

No wonder Lottie had been so desperate for him to leave. The sooner he got this matter in hand the better.

Yanking open the door to his car, he threw

himself into the back seat. 'Take me home, John,' he said curtly.

Home. He almost laughed out loud. What did he know about the concept of home? He'd lived in many houses in numerous countries, with various combinations of parents and step-parents. And now that his wealth had become something managed by other people he owned properties around the globe. Truthfully, though, despite their scale and glossy interiors, none was somewhere he felt relief when he walked through the front door.

No, there was only one place he'd ever considered home, and ironically the person who owned it was not related to him by either blood or marriage.

But he would make certain his child had the home he'd been denied.

The next morning Ragnar woke early.

It was still dark when he got up, but he knew from experience that he wouldn't get back to sleep. He dressed and made his way downstairs to the gym, and worked the machines until his body ached.

An hour later, having showered and changed, he lay sprawled on a sofa in one of the living rooms. There were eight in total, but this was the one he preferred. He let out a long, slow breath. Outside it was raining, and through the window all he could see was the dark glimmer of water and the occasional crooked outline of antlers as the red deer moved silently across the lawns.

The deer had come with Lamerton House, the Jacobean mansion and forty-acre estate that he used as a stopover when he was meeting bankers and investors in London. His gaze narrowed. They were less tame than reindeer, but the grazing herd still reminded him of home.

Home—that word again.

He stared irritably out of the window into the darkness. Normally it was a word that just didn't register in his day-to-day vocabulary, but this was the second time in as many hours that he'd thought it. His refocused his eyes on his reflection—only it wasn't his face he could see in the glass but his daughter's, so like his own and already so essential to him.

He might only have discovered her existence forty-eight hours earlier, but his feelings about Sóley were clear. She deserved a home—somewhere safe and stable. Somewhere she could flourish.

His fingers clenched against the back of the

sofa. If only his feelings about Lottie were as straightforward. But they weren't.

At first he'd wanted to blame her for so carelessly unbalancing his life, and then for keeping the truth from him, only how could he? He was as much to blame on both counts. Nor could he blame her for resenting his heavy-handed offer of money. Having managed alone for the best part of two years, of course she'd feel insulted.

But acknowledging his own flaws didn't absolve hers. She was stubborn and inconsistent and irrational. His mouth thinned. Sadly acknowledging her flaws didn't change the facts. Being near Lottie made his body swell with blood and his head swim. He had felt it—that same restless, implacable hunger that had overtaken him that night. A hunger he had spent his life condemning in others and was now suppressing in himself...

Six hours later he stood watching the dark blue saloon move smoothly along the driveway towards the house. From the upper floor window he watched as his driver John opened the door. His heart started a drumroll as Lottie slid from the car and, turning, he made his way downstairs.

As he reached the bottom step she turned and gazed up at him.

There was a moment of silence as he took in her appearance. She was wearing jeans and a baggy cream jumper. Her cheeks were flushed and her hair was tied back with what looked like a man's black shoelace. For no accountable reason he found himself hoping profoundly that the owner of the shoe in question was her brother. Raising his eyes, he turned towards John and dismissed him with a nod, so that his voice wouldn't give away the sharp, disconcerting spasm of jealousy that twisted his mouth.

'You made good time,' he said.

She nodded, her soft brown eyes locking with his—except they weren't soft, but tense and wary. 'Thank you for sending the car. It was very kind of you.' Her gaze moved past him and then abruptly returned to his face. 'So what happens next?'

It wasn't just her voice that upped his heartbeat. Her words reverberated inside his head, pulling at a memory he had never quite forgotten.

So what happens next?

Twenty months ago she had spoken the exact same sentence to him in the street outside that restaurant, and briefly he let his mind go back to that moment. He could picture it precisely. The tremble of her lips, the way her hair had spilled over the collar of her coat, and then the moment when he had lowered his mouth to hers and kissed her.

His body tensed. It had been so effortless. So natural. She had melted into him, her candid words, warm mouth and curving limbs offering up possibilities of an intimacy without the drama he had lived with so long. But of course he'd been kidding himself. Whatever it was that had caused that flashpoint of heat and hunger and hope, it had been contingent on the preordained shortness of its existence.

With an effort he blocked out an image of her body gleaming palely against the dark, crumpled bedding...

'We talk,' he said simply. 'Why don't we go and get something to drink?'

In the kitchen, his housekeeper Francesca had left tea and coffee and some homemade biscuits on the granite-topped breakfast bar.

'Take a seat.' He gestured towards a leather-covered bar stool. 'Tea or coffee? Do you have a preference?'

'Tea. Please. And I prefer it black.'

He held out a cup and, giving him a small, stiff smile, she took it from him.

She took a sip, her mouth parting, and he felt his body twitch in response. It felt strange—absurdly, frustratingly strange—to be handing her a cup of tea when part of him could still remember pulling her into his arms. And another part was hungry still to pull her into his arms again.

He cleared his throat. 'So, shall we get on with it?'

He heard the shift in her breathing.

'I accept that Sóley is my daughter, but obviously that isn't going to satisfy my lawyers, so I'm afraid I need to establish paternity. It's quite simple—just a sample from me and you and Sóley.'

There was a short silence, and then she nodded. 'Okay.'

'Good.' His gaze held hers. 'Long-term I'll be looking at establishing custody rights, but initially I just want to spend a bit of time with my daughter.' And provide a structure and a stability that he instinctively knew must be lacking in her life.

'Meaning what, exactly?'

The flicker in her gaze held the same message as the rigidity in her jaw but he ignored both.

'Since everything took off with the app I've tried to take a couple of weeks off a year—three at most—just to recharge my batteries.'

'And...?' Her eyes were fixed on his face.

'And now seems like a good time for that to happen. Obviously it's just a short-term fix, but it would give me a chance to get to know Sóley and find out what's in her best interests.'

Her expression stiffened. 'I think *I* know what's in her best interests.'

'Of course. But circumstances have changed.' He waited a beat. 'This is just a first step. I understand that there's going to be a lot to work through, and naturally any future arrangements will take into account Sóley's needs—her well-being comes first.'

Lottie stared at him in silence. 'In that case, it's probably easier if you come to me,' she said finally. 'Coming here is quite a long way for a day trip.'

He frowned. 'I wasn't expecting you to come here, and I wasn't talking about a day trip.'

'I don't understand...' she said slowly.

'Then let me explain. The whole point of these weeks is to give me time to think, to unplug myself. That's why I go back to Iceland. It's a less hectic, more sedate way of life, and it's easier to take a step back there. I'd like Sóley to go with me.'

Her eyes slipped across his face, once then twice, as though searching for something. 'You're joking, right?'

'About getting to spend some time with my child? Hardly.'

He watched his put-down meet its target, as he'd intended it to. Colour was spreading over her cheeks.

'She doesn't have a passport,' she countered tonelessly.

'But she has a birth certificate.'

Her single, reluctant nod looked almost painful.

'Then it won't be a problem. I have people who can expedite the paperwork.'

Her face seemed to crack apart. 'No, this is not happening. She doesn't know you—and she's never been anywhere without me.'

He could hear the tension in her voice and unaccountably felt himself respond to it. How could he not? She was scared. Of him. Not physically, but of his claim, both moral and legal, on their daughter, and he couldn't help but understand

and empathise with her. She had carried Sóley for nine months and cared for her on her own for another eleven. Now he was here in her life and everything was going to change.

His back stiffened. He knew exactly how that felt—the dread, then the confusion and the compromises—and for a few half-seconds he was on the verge of reaching out to comfort her. But—

But it was best not to confuse what was actually happening here. Lottie would adapt, and what mattered was agreeing the best possible outcome for Sóley.

'Clearly I was expecting you to join us.' He spoke patiently, as though to a confused child, but instead of calming her his words had the opposite effect.

'Me? Go away with you?' She shook her head. 'No, that isn't going to happen.'

'Why not? I spoke to the woman at the gallery and you have no upcoming exhibitions.'

'You spoke to Georgina?' The tightness in her face broke into a spasm of outrage. 'How dare you? How dare you talk to people behind my back?'

The note of hysteria in her voice made his shoulders pinch together. 'You're being ridiculous.'

'And you're being overbearing,' she snapped. 'You can't just expect me to drop everything.'

'Oh, but I can—and I do. And if you won't then I will have to apply a little pressure.'

'And do what, Ragnar?' She pushed up from the bar stool, her hands curling into fists, two thumbprints of colour burning in her cheeks. 'Are you going to send round your head of security? Or maybe you could kidnap us?'

How had this spiralled out of control so quickly?

He felt a familiar mix of frustration and fatigue.

'This is getting us nowhere—and in case you've forgotten, you got in touch with me.'

He stared at her in exasperation and then wished he hadn't. Her hair was coming loose and he had to resist the urge to pull it with his fingers and watch it tumble free.

He waited a moment, and then tried again. 'Look, Lottie. You go where Sóley goes. That's a given. And by pressure I just mean lawyers. But I don't want to escalate this. I just want to do what's best for our daughter. I think you do too, and that's why you came to find me the other day.'

There was a small beat of silence.

'I do want what's best for her, but…' She hesitated. 'But going away with you… I mean, three weeks is a long time for two strangers to spend together.'

There was another pulse of silence. His heart was suddenly digging against his ribs.

'But we're not strangers, are we, Lottie?' he said softly.

The silence was heavy now, pressing them closer.

Her pupils flared like a supernova and he felt his breathing stall in his throat. A minute went by, and then another. They were inches apart, so close that if he reached out he could touch her, pull her closer, draw her body against him…

And then above the pounding of his heart he heard her swallow.

'Okay. Sóley and I will come to Iceland with you.' Her expression hardened. 'And then she and I will go home. Without you.'

CHAPTER THREE

LOTTIE AND LUCAS started their walk, as they always did, by climbing over the stile in the wall at the back of the garden. After days of rain, not only was the sun shining but it was unseasonably warm.

'Usual route?' Lucas said, steadying himself on the top of the stile.

She nodded. 'But maybe come back by the river? There might be some ducks for Sóley.'

She glanced up to where her daughter sat, clapping her hands triumphantly in the backpack on Lucas's shoulders. She was wearing a lightweight purple all-in-one and a tiny knitted hat shaped like a blackberry, complete with leaves and a stalk, and in the pale lemon sunlight her skin looked as smooth and luminous as a pearl.

They trudged around the edge of the field across short, stubby tufts of grass to the lane that skirted the farmland. Instead of the usual hum of machinery, or the pensive bleating of sheep, it

was still and peaceful, but Lottie didn't mind—
her head was noisy enough as it was.

Ragnar had been on television again last
night, on some panel show and, watching him
talk about global expansion and emerging mar-
kets, she had felt a little sick. He had sounded
cool, driven and utterly focused on his goals.
Of course he'd been talking about his business,
but she could easily imagine him applying the
same focus and determination to getting what he
wanted when it came to his daughter. Plus, he
had all kinds of resources at his disposal. Look
at how quickly and smoothly he'd acquired a
passport for Sóley.

She felt her pulse jerk forward. So quickly, in
fact, that this time next week all three of them
would be flying to Reykjavik.

It was difficult to say which was more terrifying. The future when her adult daughter would
be able to travel outside of England without her
made her skin grow tight with panic, but thinking about spending three hours with Ragnar, let
alone the three weeks she had agreed to, set off
a pinwheel of alarm in her chest.

To say that she didn't want to go was the mother
of all understatements—only what choice did she
have? She could refuse, but then he would sim-

ply make good on his threat to escalate matters through the courts. Or she could go into hiding. Izzy knew loads of people who lived off-grid in houseboats and artists' communes. Only she couldn't stay hidden for ever.

Her stomach tightened.

She was just going to have to accept that it was happening.

But it was all moving so much more quickly than she'd expected.

It wasn't that she blamed Ragnar for wanting to get things rolling. If she'd been in his position she would have felt just the same. And nor did she really regret her decision to tell him about Sóley. But even though she knew she'd done the right thing, seeing him with Sóley, feeling the imperative weight of the connection between them, was making her head spin.

She felt a longing to snatch her daughter away and hold her close, and yet at the same time a longing to be part of the golden warmth of their inner circle. It was so confusing. She wanted to feel happy for her daughter, not panicky and envious, and she knew that she was being illogical, but she still couldn't stop herself from feeling just a tiny bit jealous of their blonde, blue-eyed bond.

A bond that would never include her.

A bond she had so spectacularly failed to achieve with her own father.

'I thought we might take Sóley into town next week. They're switching on the Christmas lights.'

It was suddenly hard to breathe. As Lucas's voice reverberated inside her head she looked up at her brother's face. It was so familiar, so reassuring, and yet she still hadn't worked out a way to tell him what was happening.

In the distance she could see the broad expanse of the marshes. Above their heads the sky was pale grey, silent and immense. It felt overwhelming, and yet in another way it was liberating, for it put everything into perspective. In comparison to something so infinite and enduring, surely her problems were puny and trifling and her secrecy superfluous?

She glanced across at her brother, seeing the scuffed patches on his leather jacket and the tiny points of stubble along his jawline, and suddenly she knew that this was it. The turning point. The moment she had been waiting for and both hoping and dreading would happen.

Up until now it had all been just in her head.

It had felt safe, contained, indefinite. But telling Lucas would make it real.

'That would be lovely,' she said carefully. 'Only I'm not going to be here.'

'Really?' Lucas frowned. 'I thought you were clear up until Christmas.'

She swallowed, or tried to, but the truth was blocking her throat, making it ache.

'I am—I was. But I'm…we're going to Iceland.'

He was staring at her now, his dark brown eyes trying to make sense of her words.

'Iceland? Wow, really?' He shook his head. 'That's pretty random. What brought that on?'

For a moment she was too busy trying out various sentences in her head to reply, but the need to share the truth was swelling inside her.

'We're going away with Sóley's father,' she said quickly. 'Just for a couple of weeks,' she added. 'So he can get to know her.'

Whatever Lucas might have been expecting her to say, it wasn't that. Her brother was difficult to shock. He was tolerant and easy-going. But she could tell that he was stunned by her words.

'I thought you didn't know who he was?' His

eyes searched her face, trying to guess at the truth of what she'd told him in the past.

'I didn't. But then I found out by accident and I went to his office and told him about Sóley. Then he invited me to his house, and we talked.'

Lucas cleared his throat. 'When was this?'

'A couple of days ago.'

His eyes narrowed with disbelief. 'What? And he just invited you to go away with him?'

'Yes.'

'And you agreed to go?'

As she nodded a slick of heat spread over her skin. Put like that it sounded crazy, but what was she supposed to say? *Actually, he didn't so much as invite me as issue a directive.*

She could imagine her brother's reaction. He would be furious—and understandably so. From his perspective it would seem she had been backed into a corner. Only his anger wasn't going to change the facts. Ragnar was Sóley's father, and he had a right to know his daughter.

Her heart skipped forward guiltily and she felt a slow creep of colour stain her cheeks. Ragnar's desire to know his daughter was not the only reason she had agreed to go to Iceland with him. That involved a different kind of desire.

Her mind went back to that moment in the

kitchen, when the anger and tension between them had slipped into something else, and the intensity of their emotions and the nearness of their bodies had resurrected the ghost of their unfinished connection with impossible speed.

Here in the cool November sunlight she could dismiss it as the result of nervousness or an over-active imagination, but alone with Ragnar it had been impossible to deny. In that moment the truth had been irrefutable. She wanted him—wanted him more than she had ever wanted any man.

But the suffocating force of that longing was one truth she wouldn't be sharing with her brother.

She glanced up at his profile. He looked calm, but she could read the confusion in the lines around his eyes and the tightening along his jaw.

'You think it's a bad idea,' she said slowly.

She watched with a mix of regret and relief as he shook his head.

'No, I'm just sulking because you didn't talk to me about it.'

Reaching out, she took hold of his hand and gave it a quick, apologetic squeeze. 'I wanted to but I was worried about what you'd say. What you and Mum would say,' she corrected herself. 'I didn't want to let either of you down.'

Lucas frowned. 'Let us down? Sóley is your daughter, Lottie. It's up to you, not me or Mum, if you want her to know who her father is.'

'I know, but you've always been so definite about it not mattering—you know, about our dads not being around—and Mum's the same.'

She thought back to her childhood, the hours spent watching Izzy's casual intimacy with men, the cool way she seduced and then discarded them without so much as a backward glance. To a child it had seemed both shocking, and eye-wateringly brutal, but as she'd grown older she had seen it as something else—something that underlined a fundamental difference between herself and her mother.

She felt his fingers tighten around hers.

'I do feel like that, but I know you don't—and that's okay. You're just not programmed that way, and I know that makes you feel left out sometimes. But you're my sister and I'm here for you and nothing can change that.'

Feeling the knot of tension in her shoulders loosen, Lottie nodded. It was a relief to tell Lucas the truth, but his fierce affirmation of their sibling bond mattered more. It was nothing new. She'd always needed reassurance of her place in her family. But since being confronted by Ragnar and Sóley's kinship she'd felt even more precariously placed than before.

'But that doesn't mean you have to rush into anything with Sóley's dad.'

They had reached the river now, and Lottie stared down into the water, her brother's words replaying inside her head as Sóley began to crow excitedly at a group of mallards sifting through the mud for insects and seeds.

'I can totally see why you'd want to,' he said slowly. 'But it's not like there's a time limit on paternity.'

Except there was, she thought. And at a certain point time ran out.

The blood pulsed inside her head as she thought back to her meeting with her own father. She had left it too late. So late that there hadn't been any room left for her in Alistair's life.

'In theory, no,' she agreed. 'But every day that passes is a day that tests that theory, and that's why I don't want to wait with Ragnar.'

As the silence stretched out between them she could hear the booming of her voice inside her head. Lucas was staring at her, and she could sense that he was replaying her words, mentally tracing back over the last few days.

Finally, he said slowly, 'Ragnar Stone is Só-ley's father.'

It wasn't a question but a statement of fact, and there was no point in pretending otherwise.

She nodded.

He tilted his head back and whistled sound-lessly. 'At least now I get why you're going to Iceland.' Hesitating, he looked her straight in the eye. 'Unless there is some other reason you and Mr Stone want to spend a few weeks together.'

Her face felt hot and tight. 'Of course there's no other reason.' She knew she sounded defen-sive and, remembering how her body grew loose with desire whenever she thought about Ragnar, she knew why. 'There's nothing between us,' she said quickly. 'This trip is about Sóley getting to know her father.'

It was hopeless. The tangle of her thoughts might just as well be written in huge letters across a billboard by the side of the road. But that was the problem. She didn't know how she felt or how she should feel—not about Ragnar, nor about going away with him and having him in her life. But if anyone could help her make sense of her feelings, it was Lucas.

'So you still like him?' Lucas said gently.

'No.' She shook her head, hesitated. 'I don't

know. Maybe—but it's not conscious. I mean, I don't actually like him as a person.'

There was a small beat of silence.

'Okay…' Lucas raised an eyebrow. 'So what *do* you like about him?'

Her heart shivered.

His skin. The curving muscles of his arms and chest. His smell. The way his hair fell in front of his eyes when he was gazing down at her. The fierce blueness of his gaze.

'I don't know,' she lied. 'It just felt good with him, that night.' She could admit that much—although that too was a lie, or perhaps an understatement.

It had felt glorious. An ecstasy of touch and taste. She had never wanted it to stop. Never wanted to leave that hotel room. Never felt so complete or so certain. Every fibre of her being, every atom of her consciousness, had been focused on the pressure of his body and the circle of his arms around her. Nothing else had mattered. And in the flushed, perfect aftermath of that night she had been so blazingly sure of him.

But now she knew she had made hasty and hungry assumptions. And by agreeing to go to Iceland was she making them again?

'Do you think I'm being stupid?'

Much as she loved her brother, they were different in so many ways. Like Izzy, Lucas was a serial monogamist. He was single-minded, and not subject to any need for permanence or emotional bondage, but he liked women and, probably because he was always so honest, they liked him. It was one of his strengths, that unflinching honesty, and she needed him to be honest with her now.

His forehead creased, and then he shook his head. 'You made Sóley together, so something was good between you.' He hesitated. 'But you need to be careful and clear about where you fit into all this. Don't complicate what's already going to be a fairly tricky situation with something that's out of your hands.'

He was right, Lottie thought as they turned away from the river. However fierce and real it might feel, letting something as fickle and cursory as physical attraction take centre stage was a risk not worth taking. Giving in to her hunger would rob her of perspective.

She and Ragnar had had their chance and they'd failed to make it work—and nothing, including the fact that they had an eleventh-month-old daughter, would change that.

* * *

As his private jet hit a pocket of what felt like hollowed-out air Ragnar felt his pulse accelerate. But it wasn't the turbulence that was making his heart beat faster. Over the last year he'd racked up enough air miles to have overcome any fear of flying. What was making his pulse race was the tiny shift in the drone of the engines.

They were making their descent. In less than half an hour they would land in Reykjavik. Then it would be a drive out to his estate on the Troll peninsula, and then finally he would be able to start getting to know his daughter.

Daughter.

The word still felt so unfamiliar, but then he hadn't expected to become a father for a long time. Maybe not ever. Only then he'd met Lottie, and in that moment when they'd reached for one another in that dark London street his life had changed for all time.

His eyes drifted across the cabin to where she sat, gazing out of one of the small cabin windows. Opposite her, Sóley lay across two seats, with some kind of frayed cuddly toy clamped against her body, her thumb in her mouth. She was asleep and, watching the rise and fall of her tiny body, Ragnar felt his chest ache.

As predicted, his lawyers had insisted on a paternity test, and as predicted it had come back positive. But as far as he was concerned no proof had been required. Sóley was his—and not just because they were so physically alike. There was an intangible thread between them, a bond that started with DNA but went way beyond it. He might have only found out about her existence a couple of days ago, but he already felt an unquestioning, all-encompassing love for her, and a sense of responsibility that was nothing like he'd ever felt before.

He felt his heart contract. She looked so small, so vulnerable, so ill-equipped to deal with the relentless chaos of life.

For chaos read *family*.

He thought about the complicated layers of parents and children—some related by blood, some by marriage—that made up his family. They were wilful and self-absorbed and thoughtless, but he loved them—all of them. How could he not? They were a force of nature, so full of life, so passionate and vital.

But ever since he could remember they had seemed to him like whirling storm clouds battering a mountain top. Oblivious to the damage they caused, they kept on twisting and raging, and in order to survive he'd chosen—if you could call it a choice—to sit out the storm. To be like the mountain and just let the winds carry on howling around him.

That had been his response as a child. Now, as an adult, he'd embraced the role of mediator and umpire. It was exhausting, often thankless, and always time-consuming. The swooping melodrama of their day-to-day disputes and dramas required the patience of a bomb disposal expert and the diplomacy of a trained hostage negotiator, but it was the only way, for it allowed him to live a life of calm and order on the sidelines.

He shifted in his seat, pressing his spine against the leather to relieve the tension in his back.

Now, though, he felt as though he was being sucked into a new vortex—a vortex that was the unavoidable trade-off for getting to know his daughter.

Across the cabin Sóley shifted in her sleep, losing her grip on her toy, and he watched as Lottie leaned forward and gently tucked the bear back underneath her arm.

By vortex he meant *Lottie's family.*

That glimpse in the gallery had been enough of an incentive for him to call his head of security and instruct him to make some discreet enquiries. The slim folder that had arrived on his desk less than twenty-four hours later had made for depressing reading. Both Izzy, Lottie's mother, and her brother Lucas seemed to live off-grid, rarely staying in one place longer than a couple of years and with no regular partners or jobs.

At least Lottie had an address, and she owned a house, but the idea of his daughter being raised in the eye of *that* particular storm made Ragnar suddenly so tense that before he knew what he was doing he had stood up and was walking across the cabin.

'May I?'

He gestured towards the empty seat opposite Sóley.

Lottie looked up at him, her light brown eyes not exactly contradicting the slight nod of her head but reserving judgement. He wondered why he had thought her eyes were boring. Right now, in the softly lit interior of the cabin, they were the same colour as the raw honey produced on his estate.

'Of course. It's your plane.'

She spoke politely, and it was tempting to take her words at face value. But, although her voice was free of any resentful undertone, he could sense she was still chafing against what she took to be his high-handed manner.

His gaze was drawn to his daughter and he felt his own stab of resentment. Sóley was so small, and yet he'd already missed so many of the imperceptible changes that had marked her growth from birth to now. So Lottie's indignation would have to wait—just as he'd had to wait to find out he was her father.

'I thought it would be simpler and more comfortable for you both to travel this way.'

He glanced around the cabin. There was space to move around and no other passengers, but Lottie's stony expression suggested she was unconvinced.

'I just want to spend time with her,' he said mildly.

She frowned. 'I'm not saying you don't, but you have a house in Surrey. I don't understand why we couldn't just visit you there.'

'As I told you—I like to take a couple of weeks off to recharge.'

'So we're working around your business schedule?' Her gaze narrowed. 'I thought this was supposed to be about our daughter and her well-being.'

He stared at her steadily, noting the paleness

of her face and the dark shadows beneath her eyes. Clearly she'd been having trouble sleeping, and without meaning to he found himself diverting his thoughts away from the evidence to the cause.

Was her insomnia solely a result of this disruption to her life? Or was something else keeping her awake?

His pulse stalled. Since she'd door-stepped him in front of his office his own nights had been uncharacteristically unsettled. Either he struggled to fall asleep, his head filling with images of Lottie's pale naked body as soon as he tried to close his eyes, or he dozed off only to wake exhausted after a night spent twitching restlessly through feverish, erotically charged dreams.

Blanking his mind of everything but the here and now, he met her gaze. 'It was and it is. Iceland is my homeland. I want my daughter to understand her connection to the country where I was born.'

'But she's not even a year old,' she protested. 'She won't know where she is.'

She was angry—and suspicious. He could hear it in her voice, see it in the set of her shoulders. But did she have to escalate her irritation into a full-blown confrontation? Was this how it was going to be every time they talked?

He felt a twinge of frustration. 'But *I* will know.' He shook his head. 'Tell me, is this you being deliberately bloody-minded? Or is it just impossible for you to accept that I might have a genuine motive for bringing my daughter here?'

'I'm not being bloody-minded,' she snapped. 'Cynical, maybe. In my experience your motives seem to have a habit of being a little shaky at best.'

'Meaning…?'

This conversation was pointless. He should be shutting it down. But he could feel his control slipping. It was something that had never happened before with any woman, but Lottie got under his skin. She made him lose the thread of his thoughts so that he felt off-balance and irresolute when normally he would be all cool, level-headed logic.

'You lied to me that night,' she said flatly. 'You had a whole agenda—all to do with test-driving your app—only you forgot to mention that to me. Just like you forgot to tell me that it was *your* app—the one *you* created. So forgive me if I don't find you or your claims very genuine.'

His jaw tightened. 'You think what happened

between us that night was some kind of Research and Development exercise?' He shook his head. 'Then you're right—you *are* cynical.'

Her eyes were suddenly blazing, frustration and fury lighting up their pupils. 'And you're manipulative and cold-blooded.'

He wanted to stay angry, and her absurd unjustifiable accusations should have made him see red, but as her gaze locked on his all he could think about was turning the fire in her eyes into a different kind of heat…a heat that would obliterate the tension and mistrust between them… the same white heat that had fused them together that night.

His heartbeat stalled and slowly he shook his head.

'Not with you. Not that night,' he said softly. 'You had all the power, Lottie, believe me.'

Her eyes widened and a flush of colour spilled over her cheekbones. They stared at one another, caught in the unbidden simmering spell of those remembered moments.

'Mr Stone, Ms Dawson, we'll be landing soon.'

His heart jump-started. It was his stewardess, Sam.

'If you could buckle up…?' She smiled apologetically. 'And I'm afraid that includes this little one too.'

'Of course.' He smiled coolly—more coolly than he felt.

His blood was still humming in his ears, and with an effort he forced his mind away from those taut, shimmering seconds of madness. The strength and speed of his unravelling was not admirable, but it was understandable. He was tired, and he had let his imagination run away with him, but in some ways that was a good thing.

The overwhelming, uncontrollable desire that had led him to act so carelessly twenty months ago was still there, and he loved his daughter. Only this was a reminder that those feelings were two opposing forces that could never and would never be reconciled.

How could they be when his body's response to Lottie might unleash the kind of emotion and disorder that was incompatible with the serenity he was so determined to give his daughter?

CHAPTER FOUR

ICELAND WAS NOTHING like Lottie had imagined.

Since their arrival two hours ago the sky had changed colour so many times she had lost count. Swollen lead-grey clouds had given way to a dazzling sunlight that turned everything golden, and then moments later the sun had been swallowed up by diaphanous veils of mist.

But if the weather was capricious, the land itself was otherworldly.

Through the helicopter window, the countryside rushing beneath her looked like another planet. Huge, smooth boulders that might have been used by giants in a game of football sat in a field that appeared to be covered in what looked like bright yellow moss, and carving a path several metres wide through the field was a thundering river.

It was beautiful and alien and intimidating.

A bit like Ragnar himself, she thought, gritting her teeth and hugging her daughter closer to her chest beneath the lap strap. Except that rocks and rivers didn't continually leave you second-guessing their actions.

Gazing through the glass, she tried to concentrate on the scenery, but the feeling of apprehension that had started low in her stomach when they'd landed in Reykjavik was now pushing up into her throat.

She had assumed—naively, as it now turned out—that Ragnar's home would be near Iceland's capital city. He hadn't said as much, but nor had there been any indication that it would be at the edge of the known earth, or at least the solid part.

A panicky furtive check on her phone had confirmed the worst. His home was on the Tröllas-kagi—the Troll Peninsula. Beyond the peninsula was only the sea, until you reached the archipelago of Svalbard, with a roughly equal ratio of humans to polar bears, and then there was nothing but open water until you arrived in the Arctic.

He might just as well be taking her to the moon.

She glanced swiftly across the cabin to where Ragnar sat, his blue gaze scanning the skyline. He was wearing slouchy jeans, some kind of insulated jacket, and a pair of broken-in hiking boots—the kind of ordinary clothes worn by an average man taking a break in a winter wilderness. But there was nothing ordinary about Ragnar—and she wasn't talking about his wealth or his glacial beauty. There was a concentrated intensity to his presence so that even when he was sitting down she could sense the languid power in the casual arrangement of his limbs.

He was not always so languid or casual.

Her pulse stuttered.

They had spent such a short amount of time together, and yet the memory of those few feverish hours had stayed with her.

She clenched her hands against the curl of desire stirring inside her.

Even before they'd left England the idea of being alone with him for three weeks had made her feel off-balance, but now that she was here his constant nearness was playing havoc with her senses. She didn't want to be affected by him, but unfortunately her body didn't seem to have got that particular memo.

She thought back to that moment on the plane. One minute they had been arguing and then the air had seemed to bloom around them, pushing them closer, holding them captive, so that for a few pulsing seconds there had been nothing except their mutual irresistible fascination.

She shivered. And now they were going to be stuck in the wilderness together, with nothing to hold them in check except their willpower.

It was tempting to throw his 'invitation' back in his face and tell him that she was going home—or at least back to civilisation in Reykjavik. But she doubted he would listen. And anyway, she didn't want to give him the opportunity to accuse her of having another temper tantrum.

Her gaze returned to the window. The land was growing whiter and the sky darker—and then suddenly they had arrived.

Clutching Sóley against her body, she stepped out onto the snow and gazed mutely at the house in front of her. Without the frenetic noise of the helicopter, the silence was so huge it seemed to roar inside her ears.

'Welcome to my home.'

She glanced up at Ragnar. He was standing beside her, his blond hair snapping in the wind, a slab of sunlight illuminating his face so that she could see the contours of his bones beneath the skin. He looked impassive and resolute, more returning warrior than CEO.

His eyes held hers for a few endless seconds, and then he said quietly, 'Let's go inside. I'll show you your rooms.'

'Home' didn't seem quite the right word, she thought a moment later, pressing her face against her daughter's cheek, seeking comfort in her warm, sweet smell. This was a lair—a secluded hideaway miles from anywhere—its white walls and bleached wood blending perfectly into the snow-covered landscape.

The interior did nothing to reduce her panic.

Partly it was the sheer scale of the rooms—her whole cottage would fit into the entrance hall. Partly it was the minimalist perfection of the decor, so different from the piles of baby clothes hanging above the stove and the stack of newspapers waiting to be recycled in her home. But mostly it was having her earlier fears confirmed.

That now she was here she wasn't going anywhere.

She was effectively trapped.

Back in England, when she'd acquiesced to coming to Iceland, she had assumed that if she changed her mind she could simply call a taxi.

Of course there was a helicopter sitting outside, like some squat snow-bound dragonfly, but she certainly couldn't fly it, and nor could she walk all the way back to civilisation with a baby.

Her eyes darted towards the huge expanse of glass that ran from floor to ceiling in the main living area. In the distance jagged snow-covered slopes stretched out towards an empty horizon. There was no sign of any habitation. No other buildings, no roads or telegraph poles. Just sky and snow and a sense of utter solitude.

'This is Sóley's room.'

They were upstairs now.

'The light is softer this side, and there's a beautiful view of the mountains.'

She turned to where Ragnar was holding open a door and stepped past him, trying to ignore the ripple of heat that spiralled up inside her as she momentarily brushed against his arm.

It was a beautiful room—the kind of pastel minimalist nursery that would feature in one of those upmarket baby magazines. There was a cot and a rocking chair, and a wicker basket piled high with soft toys. Unlike the rest of the house, it wasn't painted in a muted shade of off-white but in a delicate lilac, exactly the same colour as the lavender that grew in the fields beyond her cottage.

But it wasn't the unexpected reminder of home that made her body and brain freeze as though she'd fallen through ice—it was the two framed prints on the wall.

'They're mine,' she said slowly.

For a minute she was too stunned to do anything more than stare, but then slowly her brain began working again.

'You bought these through Rowley's?'

Ragnar nodded.

She stared at the prints, her heart beating out of time. It felt strange, seeing her work here in this house. Stranger still that he should have bought them unseen. But that must be what had happened, because he hadn't arrived at the gallery until later that day.

Georgina's voice floated up from somewhere inside her head. *'You know what these collectors are like. They love to have the cachet of buying up-and-coming artists' early work.'*

And she was right. A lot of wealthy buyers treated art as a commodity, and got a buzz from seeing the price of their investment soar, but...

Her arm tightened around her daughter's re-assuring warmth as a chill ran down her spine.

But those buyers hadn't had a one-night stand with the artist and got her pregnant.

Her skin was suddenly too hot and too tight, and she knew without question that Ragnar hadn't bought her work as an investment. It was something far more subtle, more insidious. He had wanted to give her money, she had refused, and so he had found another, more circuitous but less overt method of getting his own way. And he got to own a little piece of her too.

'I'll pay you back.'

Her voice sounded tense and raspy with emotion, but she didn't care. What mattered was making him understand that she was not going to be outmanoeuvred by him or his wealth.

'Maybe not right at this moment, but when we get back to England.'

His gaze skimmed her face, a muscle pulling at his jaw. 'Excuse me?'

'For the prints. I told you before that I didn't want your money—well, I don't need your charity either. Whatever it might suit you to think, I'm not some starving artist living a garret.'

As she finished speaking Sóley twisted against her, arching her back and reaching out towards the floor. She had noticed a brightly coloured octopus peeking out of the toy basket and wanted to get closer. Grateful for a reason to break eye-contact, Lottie leaned forward and let her daughter scrabble forward onto the floor.

'I see.'

There was a short silence, and then he said quietly, 'Can I ask you something? Is this how it's always going to be? Or is there the slightest chance that you can imagine a future where I can say or do something innocuous and you won't immediately put two and two together and make five?'

She looked up, her stomach swooping downwards in shock. 'What do you mean?'

'I mean,' he said softly, 'that I didn't buy your work out of charity. I came to the gallery in the morning, only you weren't there and so I had a look around. I wasn't planning on buying anything, but then I saw these, and the collage, and I changed my mind.'

Lottie stared at him in silence, her mind replaying the events of that day. There had been some kind of signal failure affecting the train on her way in and she hadn't got to the gallery until mid-morning. And when she'd arrived Jem, the gallery's co-owner, had been frantic. Georgina had swanned off to meet her latest boyfriend for a champagne brunch and he was supposed to be on the other side of London meeting a client…

As though sensing the route of her thoughts, Ragnar gave her a brief, wintry smile. 'I called Rowley's on the way back to the office,' he continued remorselessly. 'And then I was in meetings all day until I came back to the gallery in the afternoon.'

He glanced down at where Sóley sat clutching the octopus triumphantly, her mouth clamped around one furry leg, her fists clenching and un-clenching with undisguised joy.

'Not that I expect you to believe me, but I bought your work for two reasons. I think they're beautiful and, more importantly, I wanted Sóley to have something of you here. I know she probably doesn't recognise your work now, but I thought that in time she will and it will mean something to her.'

Her face was burning. A hard lump of shame was sitting heavily in her stomach and she felt slightly nauseous. She had been so certain that his motives were self-serving, only now it appeared that the complete opposite was true.

But how was she supposed to guess that he would do something so unselfish? So far their interaction had amounted to one night of feverish passion and several tense stand-offs, and from those encounters she had learned what? That the man standing in front of her was a generous, intuitive lover, but that he also had a resolve as hard and cold as the ice gullies that ran through the granite hills of his homeland.

It was all so contradictory and inconclusive.

But either way it didn't change the facts. She had jumped to conclusions and she'd been wrong.

Taking a breath, she made herself meet his gaze. 'I'm sorry, and you're right. I overreacted. It was a kind impulse.' She cleared her throat. 'And I'm not deliberately trying to make things difficult between us—ouch!'

Twin hands were gripping her leg and, glancing down, she saw that Sóley had discarded the octopus and was now trying to pull herself upright.

'Is she walking yet?'

She shook her head, relieved at the sudden change of subject. 'Nearly. She has a walker at home—you know, with wheels—and if I help her she can push it for a couple of steps.'

As though to prove the point, Sóley lifted up her foot and, holding it aloft, she stood wobbling unsteadily on one leg, before lowering it carefully onto the rug like a pony doing dressage. She tried the other leg but this was less successful, and she slid down onto her bottom, her lower lip crumpling.

'Come here then.' Lottie reached down, but her daughter had other ideas, and she watched, her heart bumping against her ribs, as Sóley crawled over to Ragnar and wrapped her arms around his legs.

'Here, let me,' she croaked.

'It's fine,' he said softly. 'May I?'

As he reached down and picked up his daughter she felt a mixture of panic and pride. For a moment Sóley looked uncertainly at Ragnar, and then, reaching forward, she buried her face against his neck, her chubby hands gripping the blond hair that curled down his neck.

Lottie felt a quick head-rush, and then her heart fluttered upwards like a kite caught in a breeze. It was the moment she'd imagined for so long—the father embracing his daughter for the first time—but nothing could have prepared her for the conflicting tangle of emotions inside her chest or the expression of fear and awe and eagerness on Ragnar's face.

Or the fact that she recognised how completely it mirrored her own reaction that first time she'd held her daughter.

'Through here is your room.'

She nodded dumbly as Ragnar gestured towards another door.

'I thought you'd want to be close to her at night.'

'Thank you.'

She managed to speak with a gratitude she knew she ought to feel—even with the briefest of glances she could see that it was a beautiful, spacious room, with the same jaw-dropping view of the mountains—and yet she was struggling to feel anything except a mounting anxiety.

His eyes were fixed on her face. 'And I'm only just down there if you need me.'

Her throat tightened and the floor seemed to tilt sharply. But why? It was a point of information, nothing more, and yet there was something in his unwavering gaze that made her pulse accelerate—a few spun-out seconds of shimmering shared memories of a different kind of need.

Terrified what her eyes would betray if she didn't move, she nodded briskly, her heart leaping with relief as Sóley made a grab for her.

'That's good to know,' she said crisply, and she stepped neatly past him, her body loosening in relief at having temporarily evaded his cool, assessing gaze.

The rest of the tour passed without any further awkward moments—partly because she was too speechless with shock to say much. She could hardly take it all in, and she hadn't even seen the indoor-outdoor geothermal pool yet, or the several thousand acres of land that made up the estate.

Pleading tiredness from the journey, she retreated to her bedroom and let Sóley explore the contents of the toy basket as she watched the light fade from the sky. It was a relief after their constant enforced proximity on the long journey to be free of that churning undercurrent of sexual tension.

But all too soon it was time for Sóley's dinner.

With all the other changes going on in her life, she wanted to keep her daughter's routines as regular as possible—particularly meal times. But venturing downstairs required a concentrated effort of will.

The cool grey kitchen was large and immaculate. Signy, Ragnar's housekeeper, showed her where everything was kept, and how to work the gleaming professional standard cooker.

'If there's anything you can't find, just tell me and I'll order it in,' she said in faultless English, beaming at Sóley.

'Thank you, but I think you've got everything already,' she said, picturing her own sparsely filled cupboards and comparing them unfavourably with the well-stocked shelves of Signy's larder.

Sóley was far less intimidated by the upgrade in her surroundings than her mother. Thrilled by her brand-new highchair, she behaved just as she did at home, thumping out a drum solo with her beaker and laughing uncontrollably as she blew peas out of her mouth.

Lottie was laughing too, so that she didn't notice Ragnar had joined them until he said quietly, 'I didn't know vegetables could be that much fun.'

She felt her heart jolt forward. Lost in the familiar rhythm of spooning peas and mashed potato into her daughter's mouth, she'd started to feel calmer. She had overreacted, but obviously being thrown together like this in a new environment, with a man she barely knew, was going to be confusing and unsettling. It was no wonder she'd got mixed up about what she was feeling.

And so what if Ragnar looked like Thor's body-double? Once she got used to having him around he would soon lose the power to make her blood catch fire.

She gave him a quick, stiff smile. 'Neither did she until last week. It's her latest trick.'

It was harder than she would have liked to shut him out. He was just so *there*—not just his actual physical presence, but that inner stillness he possessed, a self-contained sense of certainty that she lacked entirely except in her art.

Her fingers felt thick and clumsy as he watched her pick up the empty bowl.

'Does she have dessert? Or is that not allowed?'

'Yes, it's allowed.'

There was a small pause and, nodding reluctantly to his unspoken question, she tried not to feel resentful or, even more ridiculously, betrayed as he picked up a spoon and her daughter obediently swallowed every mouthful of the yoghurt she gave him.

They were bonding, and that was what she'd wanted to happen, so why did it hurt so much? Maybe seeing them together was a reminder of how she'd failed to connect with Alistair. Or perhaps, having been briefly the sole focus of Ragnar's gaze, it stung to be in the shadows.

Her chest felt tight.

She hated herself for feeling like this—and him too, for stirring up all these ambivalent, unsettling emotions. Suddenly she wanted to be somewhere far away from his orbit. Reaching down, she undid Sóley's safety harness and lifted her out of the chair.

'I'm going to take her up now and get her ready for bed.'

She sensed that he was waiting for an invitation to join them, and she knew that she was being mean-spirited by not offering him one, but she couldn't make the words form in her mouth. For a moment she thought he would challenge her, but instead he just nodded.

'I'll come up and say goodnight in a bit.'

Normally Sóley loved bathtime, but tonight her eyes were already drooping as Lottie started to undress her, and she had barely finished half her regular bottle of milk before falling asleep.

Turning down the lights, she carefully transferred her sleeping daughter to the cot. But where was her bear? Lottie frowned. Mr Shishkin had been a gift from Lucas—Sóley couldn't sleep without him. Quickly she reversed her steps, but he wasn't in the bathroom, or on her bed.

As she walked back into her daughter's bedroom her feet faltered. Ragnar was leaning over the cot.

'What are you doing?' Her heart was beating like a snare drum.

He straightened up, his eyes meeting hers in the semi-darkness. 'I found him downstairs.' He held something out to her, and she realised what it was. 'I noticed she was pretty attached to him on the flight and I thought she might need him to sleep. Or is it a her? I didn't actually look.'

She hesitated, and then saw a faint smile tug at the edges of his mouth, and even though she knew that there were no actual butterflies in her stomach, she finally understood what people meant by that phrase, for it felt as though hundreds of them were fluttering up inside her, each beat of their wings triggering a warm, tingling pulse of pleasure.

'No, it's a he. He's called Mr Shishkin.'

Feeling his curious gaze, she felt her face grow warm.

'After Ivan Shishkin, the Russian artist.' Her eyes met his. 'It's a long story, but when I was about fourteen Lucas went to Russia with some mates and he sent me this postcard of a painting of some bears climbing in a wood by Shishkin. And then he gave Sóley the bear when she was born, so...' She cleared her throat. 'Anyway, thank you for bringing him up.'

Smiling stiffly, she edged past him and, leaning forward, tucked the bear under her daughter's arm.

'You don't need to thank me. In fact, I should probably be thanking you.'

She looked up at him in confusion. 'For what?'

He held open the door, then closed it gently behind her.

'For letting me in. I know it can't be easy for you—sharing her with me, letting me get close to her—so thank you. And, if I didn't say so before, thank you for telling me about her. If you hadn't done that…if you hadn't put your personal feelings to one side… I would never have known about her.'

He meant what he was saying. She could hear it in his voice. But that wasn't what was making her skin tingle.

'What do you mean, my personal feelings?' she asked slowly.

He studied her for a few half-seconds. 'I mean that you don't like me very much.'

'I— That's not— It's not that I don't like you. I just don't…' She hesitated.

'You don't trust me?' He finished the sentence for her.

There was a small, strained pause. 'No, I suppose I don't.'

He waited a moment. 'I can understand that. But if this is going to work—you and me and Sóley—I want that to change, and I'm going to do whatever it takes to make it change, to make you trust me. And I think the best way to achieve that is by talking and being honest with one another.'

She stared at him mutely. The blue of his eyes was so clear and steady that she could almost feel her body leaning forward to dive into their depths.

'Why don't we make a start over dinner?'

Her pulse twitched, and she took an unsteady step backwards.

Dinner. The word whispered through her head, making her think of soft lights and warm red wine, and his fingers moving through her hair, and his mouth tracing the curve of her lips, stealing her breath and her heartbeat...

'I was planning on getting an early night,' she said carefully. 'It's been a long day.'

His eyes fixed on hers.

'Not for Iceland,' he said softly. 'Please, Lottie. We can eat and talk at the same time. And Signy has already prepared the food.'

Lottie hesitated, but who could resist an invitation offered up so enticingly?

An hour later, with the entire uninspiring contents of her suitcase lying on the bed, she was starting to regret her decision. It wasn't that she cared what Ragnar thought—not really—it was just hard working out what to wear. At home in her draughty cottage with Lucas she just put on more layers, but Lucas was her brother. Then again she didn't want to look as if she was trying too hard.

In the end she settled for pale grey skinny jeans and a black cable-knit sweater, smoothing her hair into a slightly more glamorous version of her usual low ponytail.

She had thought they'd eat in the kitchen, but instead she found a table set for two in the dining area of the huge living space. The table was striking, made of some kind of industrial material—carbon fibre, maybe. It looked more like a piece of an aircraft than something you would dine around. But clearly it was a table, and it was set for dinner.

She breathed out unsteadily.

Dinner for two.

Only not some heavy-handed, candlelit cliché.

There was a soft, flickering light, but it came from a huge, slowly rotating, suspended black fireplace that she didn't remember seeing before, although obviously it must have been there. But maybe her mind was playing tricks on her, because the furniture looked different too—less angular and stark, more enticing…

She shivered. Of course everything familiar looked a little different in the shadows.

Ragnar was standing at the edge of the room. He looked like a monochrome portrait, his black jeans and sweater contrasting with the bleached gold of his hair and stubble, and she felt her body loosen with desire as he walked slowly towards her.

'Are you hungry?'

She stared at him, dry-mouthed, her unspoken hunger for him blocking out the ache in her stomach, and then she nodded. 'Starving.'

His eyes met hers, the pupils black and the irises blue like bruises. 'Then let's eat.'

The meal was simple but delicious.

Mussels with butter and birch, lamb with caramelised potatoes, and a burnt bay leaf ice-cream. She wasn't usually bothered about wine, but Ragnar's wine was exceptionally drinkable.

They both made an effort to avoid conversational pitfalls, so that despite her earlier reservations she found herself relaxing. Ragnar really wasn't like any other man she'd ever met. In her experience men either had no small talk at all, or pet subjects which they returned to again and again like homing pigeons. But, although his responses were brief, Ragnar was happy to talk about anything.

Mostly, though, he wanted to talk about their daughter.

As Signy cleared away the plates, he leaned back against his chair, his blue eyes resting on her face. 'It must have been hard, bringing up a baby on your own and being a professional artist at the same time. But I want you to know that you're not alone any more. I'm here to support you in whatever way I can.'

Trying to ignore the prickle of heat spreading across her skin, she met his gaze. An hour ago she had been feeling threatened by how easily Ragnar had been accepted by their daughter, but now it felt good to know that he would be there beside her.

'Thank you. But please don't think it was all bad. Like I said before, my family have been great, and Sóley's very easy going. She's more like Lucas than me in that way.'

His face stiffened, and her stomach clenched as briefly she wondered why, but before she had a chance to speculate he said softly, 'So how is she like you?'

She felt her face tighten. It was a question that had never occurred to her. Raising Sóley as a single parent, she'd never thought about her own genetic input. It had been a given. Now, though, she could feel that certainty slipping away. *How was her daughter like her?* Physically Sóley looked just like Ragnar, and character-wise she seemed to have Lucas's sunny, open temperament.

'I don't know,' she said slowly, flattening her hands against the table to stop them from shaking.

Her heart was beating too fast, and she felt a slippery sense of panic, as though she was looking through the wrong end of a telescope, watching herself shrink.

'I do.'

She glanced up, Ragnar was staring at her steadily.

'She has your focus. She even has the same little crease here...' reaching across the table, he touched her forehead lightly '...when she's concentrating.'

Her heart was still beating too fast, only this time not in panic but in a kind of stunned happiness. Ragnar was right. She did screw up her face when she was concentrating. And the fact that he'd made the connection made her breath catch in her throat.

'She doesn't just look at things, or people, she

really gives them her whole attention. It's like she's already realised that there's something else there—some kind of "other" that she can't see.'

His fingers moved gently through her hair, then lower to her face, and his touch felt so warm and solid and irresistible that suddenly she was pressing her cheek against his hand.

She felt his hand tremble and, looking up into his face, she saw herself in the black of his pupils, saw her need and want reflected in his eyes and the same desire reflected back into hers, so that it was impossible to separate her hunger from his.

Her pulse scudded forward.

Behind her and around her the lights seemed to be spinning like a carousel, and she felt both warm and shivery. She must have drunk too much wine. But, glancing down, she saw that her glass was full. And then she looked up at Ragnar and felt her breathing change tempo as she realised that he was the source of her intoxication.

She reached shakily for the carafe of water but he was too fast.

'Here let me.'

He handed her a glass and she took it, being careful not to let her fingers touch his.

'I'm sorry... I think I must be tired.'

'We can leave dessert if you want.' As she nodded, he reached into his pocket and pulled out an envelope. 'I want to give you this. It's not urgent, but I'd like you to take a look at it when you've got a moment.'

She stared dazedly at the envelope. 'What is it?'

His eyes were a chilling, glacial blue. 'It's a letter from my lawyers—a kind of synopsis of my future relationship with Sóley.'

Her lungs felt as though they were on fire. Slowly she gazed across the room, seeing the soft lighting and glowing log fire as though for the first time.

She was such an idiot. All that talk about her seeing beneath the surface and here she was, oblivious to what was going on in front of her nose.

Her hands clenched around the stem of the glass. He'd even told her his plans.

I'm going to do whatever it takes to make you trust me.

And, like all successful businessmen, he'd identified her weak spot and then used the most effective weapon he had to exploit it and so achieve his goal. It just so happened that they were one and the same thing. *Himself.*

She felt numb. She had let her guard down, and all the time he'd been cold-bloodedly pursuing his own agenda. He might have talked about support, but he wanted control.

She thought back to when he'd showed her Sóley's bedroom. Distracted by the sight of her own artwork, she'd missed the bigger picture.

The beautifully decorated room had been a message, spelling out the future—a future in which her daughter would be picked up by a chauffeur-driven car and taken by private jet to spend time with her father. Trips that would not include her.

Her heart contracted. Why did this keep happening? She had gone to meet her father and found she was superfluous. And now, having introduced her daughter to Ragnar, he was trying to push her out of Sóley's life.

Her heart began to beat hard and high beneath her ribs.

Well, he could think again.

Plucking the envelope from his hand, she stood up. 'I'll pass it on to my own lawyer.'

She was bluffing, of course. She didn't have a lawyer. But she wanted him to feel what she was feeling—to experience, if only for a moment, the same flicker of panic and powerlessness.

Watching his face darken, she turned and walked swiftly out of the room, trying to stifle the jerky rhythm of her heart, wishing that she could walk out of his life as easily.

CHAPTER FIVE

WATCHING LOTTIE STALK out of the room, Ragnar felt as though his head was going to explode. Had that just happened? He couldn't quite believe that it had, but then it was all a completely new experience for him.

Not someone flouncing off like a diva. That had been practically a daily occurrence during his childhood. Only back then, and even more so now, he had never been a participant in the drama.

Although with Lottie he kept getting sucked in and dragged centre stage.

And now she'd walked off in the middle of everything, leaving him mouthing his lines into thin air.

A part of him was desperate to go after her and demand that she act like the grown-up he and their daughter needed her to be—but what would be the point if he didn't know what he was going to say? And he didn't.

What was more, he had no idea how an evening which had started so promisingly had ended with her turning on him like a scalded cat.

Leaning back in his chair, he rubbed his hand over his face. Her reaction made no sense.

Earlier, outside their daughter's bedroom, when they'd talked about the future, he'd made it clear that he wanted to be honest with her and she'd seemed completely on board. In fact it had been the first time since their lives had reconnected that the conversation had felt ordinary and less like the verbal equivalent of a boxing match.

Agreed, his timing with the letter could have been better, but he had thought that she'd actually started to relax a little over dinner.

He glanced across to her empty chair. He had liked it that she had started to relax, for it had reminded him of the evening when they'd first met.

His pulse quickened.

It was strange. In real terms they had spent such a short time together—so short, in fact, that it could be comfortably counted in hours. And yet the memory of it had been imprinted in his head, so that it already felt as if he'd known her a lifetime.

His mind went back to the moment he'd first seen her. She had looked just like her profile picture on the app, and yet nothing like it. Her hair was a kind of mid to light brown, but the camera lens hadn't picked up all the lustrous threads of gold and copper, and nor had it caught the softness of her eyes or the sweetness of her tentative smile. But mostly, because of course it was only a photo, it had failed to capture that mesmerising husky voice.

Frankly, she could have been reading the phone book backwards to him and he wouldn't have noticed. And it had been the same earlier, as she'd talked about their daughter.

He hadn't wanted to break the spell. In fact, he hadn't been able to break it. Truthfully, he had been fighting himself all evening not to lean across the table and kiss her. But there was no point now in imagining how it would feel to have those soft lips part against his and, picking up his wine glass, he drained the contents.

Standing up, he switched off the lights and made his way upstairs. As he reached the top step he hesitated.

His rooms were to the right, but from where he was standing he could see a thin line of light beneath Lottie's door. Instantly he felt his breath clog his throat. She was awake, and they definitely had unfinished business. Before he had a chance to finish that thought, he was turning to the left and walking towards her room.

He reached her door in three strides and raised his hand—but as he did so he caught sight of the illuminated numerals of his watch and something…a sharp memory of nights spent listening to the sound of raised voices and doors slamming…stayed his hand. Instead of knocking, his knuckles brushed soundlessly against the wood.

It was after midnight. The house was in darkness.

More importantly, this wasn't him. He watched, he waited, but he didn't participate. He certainly didn't ever walk into a storm of his own volition, and there was nothing to be gained by doing so now.

Restarting their tense conversation in the more intimate setting of her bedroom had 'bad idea' written all over it in mile-high letters. It would be far better to wait until the morning to confront her—not least because their strongest motive for any reconciliation would be awake and eating breakfast in her highchair.

Turning, he walked to his room. It was late, and he was tired, and his body was aching as though it was going through some kind of withdrawal.

He needed a quick shower and a long sleep—
not some protracted debate with someone who
was just going to argue that black was white.

Besides, she was probably already in bed.

He breathed in sharply, his groin hardening in
the time it took his brain to jump from thinking
the word 'bed' to picturing a near naked Lottie
between the sheets.

Was this his fault?

He couldn't see how. The evening had been
going so well. They'd eaten and talked, and
watching the way her eyes shone with eagerness when she talked about Sóley had made his
breathing lose rhythm. Only when he'd asked
her how she was like her daughter the joy had
faded from her voice and her fingers had started
to shake as if someone was pressing a bruise on
her heart.

He hadn't thought about what he was going
say or do—in fact he hadn't been thinking at all.
He had felt her pain, and he'd wanted to make
whatever it was that was hurting her stop, and
so he'd reached out and touched her face, half
expecting her to pull away.

Only she hadn't. And then, watching her eyes
soften, he had been lost, falling back to that night
when the softness in her eyes had stripped him

not just of his clothes but of all sense and inhibition.

His body tensed—not at the memory of Lottie's hands pulling at the buckle of his trousers, but at the dull, insistent hum of his phone.

Glancing over to where it lay on the bed, he cursed softly. It would be Marta, his nineteen-year-old half-sister. She was the youngest member of his family and for the last two months had been holding off all rivals in a crowded field to take the title of most demanding sibling in his life.

His jaw tightened. He loved his sister, but since the acrimonious breakdown of her parents' marriage her life had been spiralling out of control. She had been stopped by the police and given a warning for reckless driving, and then she and her now ex-boyfriend Marcus had been involved in an argument with some photographers, after his twenty-first birthday party. And all of it had been gleefully reported in the media.

What she needed was guidance and reassurance.

What she had was a father—Nathan, who had already moved on to a new actress-model wife, and was wrapped up in the imminent birth of their first child.

She also needed her mother—who also happened to be *his* mother. Except Elin was far too busy being placated by her entourage of hairdressers and personal trainers to deal with her difficult daughter.

Only why did that make Marta his problem?

But he knew why. He couldn't turn his back on his family, and nor could he live like them, so the only way he could make it work was by taking a step back—just as he'd done outside Lottie's door.

He thought back to when Marta was a little girl. She had always been bringing him some necklace or bracelet that was so snarled up it was impossible to see where it began and where it ended, but he'd always sat down and patiently untangled it for her. It was just what he did—what he was still doing. Only now it was her life that he was untangling.

'Marta—'

He heard her quick breath, like a gasp, and then she was speaking incoherently, fat, choking sobs interspersing every other word.

'Ragnar—Ragnar, I hate her! She won't listen to me. It's not my fault. I can't stand living with her. You have to speak to her.'

She burst into tears.

Pushing back against the surge of tiredness swirling around him, Ragnar walked slowly across the room and stopped in front of the window, wondering exactly what had triggered this latest set-to between his mother and half-sister, and whether she had even considered the possibility that he might be sleeping.

Almost certainly not, he thought, gazing up at the sky. It was a clear night, and his brain ticked off the constellations as he waited for her to stop crying. When, finally, she let out a juddering breath he said calmly, 'Better? Okay, tell me what's been going on.'

It was a fairly straightforward story from Marta's point of view. In her telling, she was the innocent victim, her mother and father were twin evil villains, and he, Ragnar, had been drafted in to play the role of rescuer.

'She's horrible all the time and I'm sick of her acting like it's all about her.'

'It's not all about her—but she has just lost her husband,' he said mildly.

His sister's tears slid into resentful fury. 'He's not dead,' she snapped. 'He's just shacked up with that hideous stick insect in Calabasas. And anyway, it's hypocritical of her to be so upset. It wasn't as though she cared when she left Frank.'

To a certain extent that was true, Ragnar conceded. Elin had discarded her fourth husband, Frank, without so much as a backward glance, but perhaps she had expected her fifth husband to be her last. Although perhaps not. His mother had the kind of blonde ethereal looks that laid waste to any man who crossed her path, and she was rarely satisfied with anything or anyone for long.

But, putting aside Marta's tears and rage, what mattered was brokering peace between her and their mother.

'I think what you both need is a bit of space from one another.'

He hesitated. Lamerton would be empty for three weeks, and in his family three weeks was the equivalent of a decade in terms of drama. Quite possibly the whole thing would have blown over by then, but in the short term getting his sister and mother on different continents would stop them killing one another.

He cleared his throat. 'Look, if you need somewhere to stay you can use Lamerton. I'm sure you'll find something to amuse you in London.' Or more likely *someone*, he thought dryly. 'And if you don't want to see anyone you can just chill out on the estate.'

'Oh, Ragnar, really? You're an angel.'

Hearing her squeal of excitement, he nearly changed his mind. An empty house miles from anywhere and an unsupervised and excitable Marta were not a good combination—but, having planted the seed, he knew that it would be impossible to dislodge the idea from her mind. He would just have to hope that her fear of getting on his wrong side would curb her worst instincts.

'This doesn't mean I don't have rules, Marta,' he said firmly. 'You will be polite to John and Francesca. They are not there to put up with your mess or your tantrums.' He paused. 'Of course ordinarily I'd tell you to treat the place as your own, but in your case—*in your case*,' he repeated over her squawk of protest, 'I would ask that you don't. And do not—I repeat, *do not*—even think about having a party. And by "party" I mean any gathering of people numbering more than you and one other person.'

There was a small sulky silence from the other end of the phone, and then he heard her sigh.

'Okay, fine. I'll be polite, and I won't make a mess, and *obviously* I wouldn't dream of having a party in your house.'

Catching sight of himself in the window, Ragnar was tempted to roll his eyes at his reflection. Instead he said calmly, 'I just don't want there to be any confusion.' Glancing down at his watch, he grimaced. It was nearly a quarter past one. 'Right, I'll leave you to talk to Elin. Just let me know when you're going over and I'll send John to pick you up.'

'Thanks Ragnar.' Her voice softened and she hesitated. 'Actually, do you think you could call her? I think she'll take it better from you.'

After he'd hung up he stood with the phone in his hand, thinking. As usual Marta hadn't asked him one question about himself, but at no point had it occurred to him to tell his sister that she was an aunt. Nor was he planning on telling her until it was absolutely necessary. He wanted to keep his daughter to himself for a while—keep her from being absorbed by his family.

He'd talk to his mother later. Now he really was going to bed.

He showered quickly, towelled himself dry and then pulled on the loose cotton trousers he wore to sleep in.

As he unfastened his watch, he heard it.

A baby crying.

He paused, his body turning instinctively towards the sound.

The wail faded and, flicking off the light, he closed his eyes and rolled onto his side, his mind sliding smoothly into sleep.

He woke with a start.

Reaching out, he found his watch in the darkness. It was just gone half-two in the morning.

But why had he woken?

And then he heard it—the same unmistakable wail as before. For a few half-seconds he lay in the darkness, listening to his daughter cry. Only this time it didn't falter. Instead it seemed to be escalating.

Had she cried like that before?

Not really. A little on the plane, but that had been more like a kind of fussing.

His chest felt suddenly leaden with tension, and he sat up and switched on the bedside light.

It was ten to three now.

Was that a long time for a baby to cry?

Why wasn't she stopping?

He tried to remember his half-brothers and sisters at Sóley's age, but all the adults in his life had always been more than happy to let a crying baby or toddler disappear with a nanny.

His pulse sped up as the baby carried on wailing. She had seemed fine earlier, but she didn't sound fine now. Her cry was changing, intensifying in pitch, so that even at this distance he could feel her distress resonating inside his chest.

And suddenly he was moving—rolling out of bed and walking swiftly out of his room.

The noise grew louder and louder as he got closer. For a moment he stood outside the door to his daughter's room, but when the crying began again he pushed it open.

Lottie was standing in the centre of the room with her back to him, wearing some kind of robe, her hair spilling over her shoulders. She was rocking the baby gently, making soothing sounds, and as he spoke her name she turned, her eyes widening with shock.

'Is everything okay?'

It wasn't. He didn't need to be a childcare expert to see that Sóley was upset and so was Lottie.

The baby's cheeks were red and tear-stained and she was burrowing against her mother's shoulder like some little mammal, then abruptly rearing backwards, her small face scrunched up in inconsolable fury.

Lottie looked pale and exhausted. 'She's teething.'

She winced as Sóley jerked her head up and

banged into her chin, and then immediately began crying again.

As her ear-splitting crescendo of rage and frustration filled the room, Ragnar took a step forward. 'Here, let me.'

'No—' Her eyes flared, and she half turned away, clutching her struggling daughter. 'I didn't ask for your help and I don't want it.'

He could hear the fatigue in her voice—and something like fear.

Only why would she be scared?

He stared at her back in silence. He didn't know the answer to that question, but he did know that he didn't like the way it made him feel.

'Lottie,' he said again. 'I know you don't need my help. Of course you don't. You've managed without it for eleven months. I'm not trying to interfere—really, I'm not. Just tell me what to do and I'll do it.'

'You can leave.' She turned, her eyes fierce. 'That's what you can do.'

He stared at her, biting down on his own corresponding rush of anger. Earlier she'd got upset about the letter from his lawyers, and now she'd turned on him like a cornered lioness with her cub—so what exactly was the right way for him to be a part of his daughter's life?

As though Sóley had heard his thoughts she lifted her head, her blue eyes fixing on his face, and then without warning she reached out for him. Shocked, he caught her, intending to return her to Lottie, but her tiny hands were already grasping his neck and he felt his heart swell against his ribs as she tucked her face against his shoulder, her sobs subsiding.

Her body felt hot and taut, but after a moment he felt her grow heavier and automatically he began to rock her in his arms, shifting slowly from side to side, holding his breath, his entire consciousness fixed on the softness of her cheek against his skin and its confirmation of his incontestable role in her life.

'Here.' Lottie was laying a blanket over her daughter's back. 'When you put her in the cot she needs to go on her side,' she said flatly.

He leaned over and placed the baby carefully on the mattress. As he slid his hands out from under the weight of her body she shifted in her sleep, her fingers splaying out like tiny pink starfish, but then she gave a small, juddering sigh, and as he tucked her bear underneath the blanket her breathing slowed and grew steadier.

He felt a rush of relief and exhilaration and, straightening up, he turned towards Lottie. It wasn't quite a team effort, but it was the first time they had worked together as parents. He wanted to share the moment with her and, stupidly, he had assumed, or hoped anyway, that she might feel the same way.

If anything, though, she looked drawn and distant, and desperate for him to leave.

His jaw tightened.

Obviously they had parted on poor terms earlier in the evening, and he would have to be emotionally tone-deaf not to see how annoying it must have been to watch Sóley settle in his arms, but surely she could take a step back and meet him halfway.

He glanced over at her small, still face.

Apparently not.

'So, I should—we should probably get some sleep,' she said stiffly.

There could be no mistaking either her tone or the implication of her words. She was dismissing him.

The skin of his face was stretched so tight he thought it might crack, and he was having to physically restrain his temper as though it was a wilful horse.

But he'd reached his day's quota of conversations with irrational childish women, and without saying a word he turned and left the room.

Watching the door close closed behind him, Lottie breathed out unsteadily.

She wanted to scream and rage like her daughter. Her whole body was jangling, aching with misery. She knew she was being unreasonable and petty, and that she should be happy that Ragnar wanted to be a hands-on father. But she hurt so badly that there wasn't room for any other feeling.

It had been such a shock, seeing Sóley reach out for him like that. Her daughter had always wanted *her*, before anyone else. Watching him settle her, she'd told herself that it didn't matter. That it was what was meant to happen and what she'd wanted to happen and that she didn't mind.

Except that she did mind.

It made her feel empty and cold, as though a huge dark cloud was blocking out the sunlight.

You're being stupid, she told herself. *You're just tired and it's making you think crazy thoughts. Sóley was exhausted. If he hadn't been there she would have settled with you.*

But that wasn't the point.

She had been there and her daughter had still

chosen Ragnar. If he'd been in her life from birth she would never have questioned it, or cared. Only having grown up without a father herself, she'd assumed that she took precedence and that his role was secondary...inferior. Optional.

She bit her lip. But those were her mother's values, not hers, so why was she behaving like this? Why invite his involvement and then keep him at arm's length?

It was all such a mess.

If only she was at home. She would go downstairs, where the range would be warm, and she would lean against it, absorbing its heat while she waited for the kettle to boil. And maybe Lucas would wake up and come and sit at the table and tell her some crazy story about his day...

She pushed back against the swell of homesickness in her throat. Thinking about family and her cottage wasn't going to help. She needed to sleep, but the thought of lying in the darkness and just waiting for her body and brain to relax was appalling. Maybe if she made herself some tea? It would mean going downstairs, but it was what she would do at home and right now she needed something familiar.

Clutching the baby monitor and using her phone as a torch, she made her way to the kitchen.

Thankfully, she remembered where the light switches were.

Signy had shown her how to use the stainless steel state-of-the-art coffee machine. But coffee was the last thing she wanted or needed.

'What are you doing?'

An electrical current snaked down her spine and her head snapped round. Ragnar was standing at the other end of the kitchen, watching her steadily.

She stared back at him, her heart bumping against her ribs. Upstairs, with Sóley screaming and her nerves in meltdown, she had not really noticed what he was wearing—or rather not wearing. Now, though, in the quiet intimacy of the kitchen, it was difficult to drag her gaze away from his smooth, muscular chest, and the trail of tiny golden hair that disappeared into the waistband of his trousers.

But never mind what he was wearing, what about her? She glanced down at herself, her skin suddenly prickling. Had her robe shrunk or did it always show this much leg?

'I'm trying to find tea bags. Signy did show me, but I can't remember.'

'I know where they are.' He walked across the kitchen. 'Any particular flavour?'

She shrugged. As soon as his back was turned she jerked the robe tighter, tugging the hem lower over her thighs. 'Chamomile. Or peppermint. I can make it myself.'

There was a moment's silence.

'I'm sure you can,' he said.

She watched as he filled a teapot with boiling water from the coffee machine.

'Here we are.' He slid a teapot onto the counter. Her eyes darted to the cups—the *two* cups.

'I thought I'd join you.' His eyes rested on her face. 'Unless you've any objections?'

Taking her silence as consent, he slid onto one of the bar stools and she jerked her eyes away from the flex of his stomach muscles. 'Would it matter if I did?'

He held her gaze. 'That would depend, I suppose, on your objection.'

She swallowed. 'You sound like a lawyer.'

He didn't flinch. 'You're not on trial here, Lottie.'

'Really?' She shook her head. 'That's not how it feels to me.'

He leaned backwards, his arm draped casually against the counter, but she caught a flash of blue and knew that he was watching her intently. 'I disagree.'

She blinked. 'Right. So you're telling me how I'm feeling?' she said slowly.

Her fingers twitched against the handle of the cup. There was something about his words that made a veil of red slide in front of her eyes. His arrogant assumption that he knew better than her. That he knew her better than she knew herself.

'That's not what I said.'

'And yet that's exactly how it sounded.' She glared at him.

He sighed. 'You know, if anyone's on trial here it's me—although I have to admit I'm not exactly sure what it is you're accusing me of doing.'

She was suddenly simmering with anger. Surely he was joking? 'Other than backing me into a corner and threatening me with lawyers at every opportunity.'

'There was nothing threatening in that letter—which you would know if you'd bothered to read it. But then why read it when you've already made up your mind?'

He spoke quietly, but she could hear a thread of exasperation weaving through his voice.

What did he have to be frustrated about?

She was the one losing control of her life and her daughter. And it was disingenuous of him to say that the letter wasn't threatening. Maybe it wasn't, but the fact that he had lawyers on call who worked out of office hours to protect his interests was intimidating, and he knew it.

'You said that you didn't want to escalate things,' she said accusingly. 'That you just want what's best for Sóley—'

'I don't.' He cut her off. 'And I do.'

'Well, I disagree.' She met his gaze, feeling a small rush of satisfaction as she threw his words back at him. 'You want what's best for you. Everything is on your terms. *Where* we met, *when* we met. *This holiday.* You even went behind my back to Georgina.'

'Out of courtesy.' His blue eyes were like chips of glacial ice. 'And if I hadn't—if I'd left it to you—I'd still be waiting to meet my daughter.'

She stared at him, open-mouthed, a beat of anger leapfrogging across her skin. He was unbelievable. How could he be so unfair? So self-righteous?

'In case you've forgotten, I was the one who got in touch with you.'

'I haven't forgotten,' he said tersely. 'I just don't understand why you bothered.'

Her hands balled into fists. 'You know why. So you could get to know Sóley.'

'Except you don't want me to get to know her.' He shook his head, his blue eyes hard and uncompromising. 'What exactly is it you want from me? You gave me such a hard time for even suggesting that I help you financially, but every time I so much as offer to hold my daughter you can't get away from me fast enough. Look at tonight,' he carried on remorselessly, 'I wanted to help and you kept pushing me away.'

Her heart was pounding. He was right. She *had* pushed him away, and from his perspective it probably didn't make sense. But why did she have to see anything from his point of view? It wasn't as though her needs were high on his agenda.

She took a deep breath. 'Do you think that was the first time she's been like that?'

'No, of course not. And I'm not questioning your parenting skills. I know you can cope, but I don't know why you think you need to cope alone.'

She felt a buzzing in her ears. Out of any question he could have asked, it was the one that hurt the most. How could she explain to this cool-eyed stranger who didn't need anyone how she felt?

Her daughter's birth had made her feel whole

and necessary. It had taken the sting out of her father's rejection and eased her ever-present sense of being 'other' to her mother and brother's dark-eyed autonomy.

And then she had seen Ragnar on television and, prompted by guilt and a desire to do the right thing, she had got in touch. Maybe it had been the right thing to do, but it felt like a mistake—only it had taken until tonight for her to see how big a mistake.

'It doesn't matter.'

Her throat tightened and she pushed back her chair. Her voice was shaking...her hands too. She wanted to leave, to crawl somewhere quiet and dark and hide from the terrible ache of loneliness that was swallowing her whole.

'It does to me.'

He was standing too now, but that wasn't what made her hesitate. It was the sudden fierceness of his words, as though they had been dragged out of him against his will.

'I have to go,' she said.

She felt his hand brush against hers.

'What is it?' he asked.

'It's nothing.' She shook her head. 'I'm just tired.'

'Tired of what?'

The gentleness of his voice as much as his question itself surprised her. 'I don't know,' she lied, lowering her face.

She couldn't tell him the truth. How could she explain the convoluted, chaotic journey that had brought her here, to this kitchen, to this man who lived his life by numbers?

But if she'd thought her silence would answer his question she'd been wrong. Glancing up, she saw that he was waiting, willing to wait for however long it took, and the fact that he was prepared to do that for her seemed to ease the tightness in her throat.

'It's stupid really...and unfair.'

'What is?' he said softly.

'It's not their fault. It's not my mum and Lucas's fault that I feel like an outsider when they're together.'

He studied her face. 'I thought you were close to them?'

'I am.' Her mouth trembled. 'I love them, and they love me, but we're so different.' She frowned. 'I know it sounds ridiculous, and I'm not expecting you to understand, but it feels like even though they're my family I don't fit in.'

For a moment he didn't reply, and then his eyes met hers. 'No, I do understand.'

She took a breath. 'I thought for a long time that I must be like my dad. My mum never told him she was pregnant with me, and I was convinced that if I met him there would be this moment of recognition, this connection between us.'

Her voice faltered, the memory of that stilted meeting catching her unawares, the feeling of failure and disappointment undimmed by time.

'But it didn't?' he asked.

She shook her head. 'It was too late. There was nothing there. We were like damp firewood.' Clenching her hands, she forced her mouth into a stiff smile. 'That's why I wanted you to meet Sóley now, when you still had room for her.'

'It wouldn't have mattered when you told me. I would always have made room for her,' he said simply, and her heart thudded hard as he caught her hands, uncurling her fists and slotting his fingers through hers. 'But that doesn't mean there isn't room for you too.'

She was about to protest, to pretend that he'd misunderstood, but then she thought back to how it had felt when her daughter had reached out to Ragnar. 'I don't want to lose her.'

'You won't.' Letting go of her hands, he gripped her shoulders. 'You can't lose her. She loves you and needs you more than anyone else in the world. You're her mother.'

'And you're her father.' Her face tightened. 'And I'm sorry that I've pushed you away.'

His gaze was the clear deep blue of an Arctic sky. 'I'm right here. And I'm not going anywhere.'

'But I've made everything so difficult—and that's not what I wanted to do...not what I want to do—'

She broke off, her insides tightening as they both listened to her words reverberate around the silent kitchen.

A minute passed, and then another.

'So, what is it, then?' he said hoarsely. 'What do you want to do, Lottie?'

She stared at him dazedly. Her tongue was in knots and she couldn't seem to breathe right. The air around her was shifting and swelling, pressing closer. She was losing her balance.

Reaching out to steady herself, she laid the palm of her hand against his chest. He breathed in sharply, his shoulders tensing, and the sudden acceleration of his heartbeat made her whole body tremble.

'What do I want?' she whispered.

For one intense, dizzying second they stared at

one another, and then she took a small, unsteady step towards him.

'I want this,' she said and, leaning forward, she kissed him lightly.

His mouth was warm and firm, and she felt her limbs turn to air as he wrapped a hand around her waist and pulled her closer, moulding her body against his.

Heat was seeping through her robe, spreading out beneath the insistent pressure of his fingers, and she moaned softly, her arms circling his neck, her hands grasping his hair as he parted her lips, deepening the kiss. She felt his hands sliding smoothly over the bare skin of thighs, and then he was lifting her up onto the counter.

The granite was hard and cold, but she barely noticed. She could feel his lips moving over her neck, his tongue circling the pulse beating at the base of her throat, and then his hands cupped her breasts, and as his fingers pushed aside the thin fabric and found her nipples she gasped into his mouth.

Her head was spinning, her abdomen aching with a tension that made her stir restlessly against him. She was so tight and damp and, grabbing his arms, she curled her legs around his thighs, drawing him closer, pushing against the solid length beneath his trousers, trying, wanting, *needing* to appease the ache—

The sudden burst of static was like a thunderclap.

They both froze, jerking backwards from one another as though they'd been stung.

Lottie clutched at the counter as the kitchen swam back into focus. What were they doing? *What was she doing?*

'Lottie—'

Ragnar was standing beside her, but her eyes were fixed guiltily on the baby monitor.

'I have to go.'

She glanced up at him. His eyes were narrowed and he was breathing unsteadily. He looked as dazed as she felt, but right now she wasn't up to sharing anything with him—particularly her shock at their sudden mutual loss of control.

She shook her head. 'I can't.'

And, still shaking her head, she snatched up the monitor and fled.

CHAPTER SIX

STANDING IN FRONT of his bedroom window, Ragnar gazed unblinkingly into the lemon-coloured light. At some point it had snowed heavily, and an eiderdown of sparkling untouched whiteness stretched away from the house as far as the eye could see.

He had woken late—so late, in fact, that in the first few seconds after he'd opened his eyes he'd struggled to remember where he was, even when it was. The last time he'd slept in late he'd been about fourteen years old.

He breathed out against the dull ache in his groin. And that wasn't the only similarity with his fourteen-year-old self. His body hardened as he rewound his mind back through the early hours of the morning, pressing 'pause' at the moment when Lottie had reached out and touched his chest and then leaned in to kiss him, or had he lowered his mouth to kiss her?

She had been wearing some kind of soft cotton robe and, catching a glimpse of her trying to smooth the fabric so that it covered more of her thighs, he had completely lost track of what she saying, for it had been all too easy to imagine those same hands smoothing and caressing his body.

But had he known what was about to happen?

He considered the question. Not in terms of seconds and minutes maybe. And yet it had been out there waiting to happen since the moment their lives had reconnected outside his office.

They'd both been fighting it, using anger to deflect their desire, but each time they'd quarrelled their hunger had edged out their anger a little more, until finally it had been too tempting, too inevitable, too impossible to resist.

Their unfinished connection was like that feeling when you found a loose tooth and couldn't leave it alone and kept probing and jiggling it with the tip of your tongue. Hardly surprising then, that they had ended up kissing.

The kiss had been fierce and tender and beyond any conscious control. A kiss driven by a need and hunger that had burned like a molten core deep inside him.

It had lasted sixty seconds at most, and yet it had felt like an admission of everything that had gone on between them. And everything that was still pulling them together now.

He breathed out unsteadily. It was the first time he'd really acknowledged that fact—that this pulsing thread of longing was as much about the present as the past. Although why it had taken him so long to figure that out was a mystery, given that he seemed to think about Lottie in all the pauses in his day and in the dark silence of the night.

To put it in its simplest terms, he wanted her— and she wanted him. But where would that wanting take them?

His heart thumped lightly against his ribs. Sex was supposed to be simple, and at its most simple it was just bodies connecting and intertwining.

He felt his body harden more.

But, of course, in reality sex was rarely that straightforward. How could it be? There were billions of people on the planet. Even if you eliminated vast numbers of them on the grounds of age, geography, or mutual attraction, that still left a lot of potential hook-ups out there—and, realistically, what were the chances of two people who felt exactly the same way about sex and commitment finding one another and then continuing to feel the same way until death parted them?

He grimaced. Judging by his family's track record: slim to none. But he already knew that. It was the reason he'd created *ice/breakr* in the first place. To mathematically optimise the odds of couples finding a match. And the numbers clearly worked. According to the latest data from his team, the app was making about twelve million matches a day.

There was just one small problem. According to his own algorithm, one night should have been enough to satisfy both himself and Lottie—and they'd already shared a night. Yet just hours ago, the strength and speed of their desire had been mutual and irresistible.

So what happened now?

He sighed. He was back where he'd started and no nearer to finding an answer.

The dull, insistent ring of his phone made him glance away from the window and the confusing, circuitous path of his thoughts. Walking over to his bed, he picked up the phone and looked down at the screen, his face stilling. It was his mother.

He'd called her earlier and left a message, suggesting that Marta should go over and stay at Lamerton. No doubt she was returning his call.

He was about to answer her when something pulled at the edge of his vision—a movement, the shape of a person, a woman…

His pulse began to beat faster, his heart leaping against his ribs as though trying to reach her.

It was Lottie, holding Sóley in her arms. Maybe it was her clothes—she was dressed for the weather in a black fur-trimmed parka and dark jeans—or maybe it was her loose ponytail and chunky dark boots, but she looked more like a student than a professional artist and mother.

He stared at her, transfixed. In the margins of his brain he knew that his phone was still ringing, but for the first time in his life he ignored it.

There was something so beautiful and tranquil about the scene outside his window, and he didn't want to risk spoiling it by letting an episode of his family soap opera play out in the background.

He felt his phone vibrate in his hand as his mother left a message. But that was fine. For once, she was going to have to wait.

His shoulders tightened. Outside the window, Lottie was holding out a handful of snow for his daughter to inspect.

His daughter.

He frowned. He should call his mother back, tell her about Sóley. Forming the words inside his head, he tried to imagine saying them to his mother. But, just as when he'd been talking to Marta, he checked himself—and immediately felt guilty, but relieved.

At some point he would tell everyone, but right now he wanted to keep his daughter to himself for a little longer—to defer the moment when she would be absorbed by his chaotic, wonderful, exhausting family.

He walked slowly beside the window, shortening his strides to mirror Lottie's as she picked her way slowly across the snow-covered lawn like one of the deer at Lamerton.

She stopped, and he stopped too. Holding his breath, he watched her lean forward and lower the little girl onto the snow. Sóley was wearing an all-in-one snowsuit, and her bright golden curls were hidden beneath a tiny hat shaped like some kind of fruit. Holding both her mother's hands, she teetered unsteadily on the spot, but even at this distance her excitement was tangible, and he felt a smile pull at the corners of his mouth as she tugged one mittened hand free and crouched down to pat the snow.

It might be the first time she'd ever seen it, and he felt a buzz of elation at witnessing her delight.

He stared intently through the glass, enjoying

this unexpected opportunity to observe mother and daughter together, all the more so because Lottie had no idea that she was being watched.

His mouth twisted.

That made it sound like he was spying on her—but was it really so bad to want this one small moment to himself? Obviously it wasn't the first time he'd seen the two of them together, but he knew his presence set Lottie's teeth on edge.

Although maybe that had changed now, he thought, remembering how she had opened up to him in the early hours of the morning.

When she'd first started talking about feeling tired he'd assumed she was referring to all the sleepless nights involved in having a small baby, but then she'd told him about her father's rejection, and her feeling of being different from her mother and brother.

Her honesty had surprised and touched him— the more so because he still regretted the lies he'd told her that first night.

But it was not just her honesty that had got under his skin.

His sisters and brothers, even his parents, poured out their hearts to him on a regular basis, but always his first instinct was to blank out the emotional drama and concentrate solely on the facts. Only with Lottie there had been no drama. She hadn't wept or raged, and yet he'd found it impossible to block out the quiet ache in her voice as she'd told him her story.

It was an unsettling discovery to meet someone who could slip beneath his defences, and for it to be Lottie was even more unnerving. Only wasn't it completely understandable for him to feel that way? Logical, even?

Lottie was the mother of his daughter, so of course he cared. He hadn't liked knowing that she was upset, or that in some clumsy way he had contributed to her distress. And it had been only natural for him to want to comfort her.

Glancing back down at the woman standing in the snow, he felt his body still, remembering the feverish kiss they'd shared. Truthfully, comforting her had been low, low down on his agenda when the blood had been pounding through his veins and he'd lowered his mouth to those sweet, soft lips.

He wanted her and she wanted him, and his heartbeat stumbled as the question came back to him—the one he'd turned away from earlier. *But where would that wanting take them?*

He wasn't a fool, and he knew that giving in

to this ache, this hunger, this pull between them, would end badly. How could it not? There was too much at stake—too much to lose or damage or both. Having sex with Lottie, no matter how badly he wanted it or she wanted it, would introduce too many random elements into their relationship, and he didn't do random.

He felt his shoulders stiffen.

More to the point, he didn't do relationships.

And here in his home, the home he was sharing with her and their daughter, sex was never going to feel like just some casual hook-up. There would be consequences—tempting to ignore now, in the face of the urgency and pull of their desire, but as he knew from personal experience of unpicking his family's destructive, impulsive affairs, they were consequences that ultimately neither of them would be able to outrun.

Consequences he didn't want to take on.

Not now, not ever.

Taking her eyes off her daughter for a moment, Lottie raised her face and gazed up at the sky. She had been hoping that it would have the same effect that it did in Suffolk, and that the feelings of inadequacy and mortification she'd been carrying on her shoulders since waking would magically melt away in the face of its vast indifference.

It might have worked if the sky had been the washed-out grey of yesterday. Unfortunately she was in Iceland, and today the sky was the same brilliant blue as Sóley's eyes—Ragnar's too.

Her heart gave a thump and she felt a thumbprint of heat on both cheeks as she thought back to what had happened and what might so easily have happened in the early hours of this morning.

She still couldn't quite believe that she'd told Ragnar about her father, and about how she felt about Lucas and her mum. But that wasn't even the worst part. As if blurting out all that wasn't mortifying enough, she'd then completely lost her mind and kissed him.

Driven by the restless ache that had been turning her inside out, she hadn't been able to hold back—and she hadn't wanted him to hold back either.

She'd crossed the line. Not in the sense of winning a race, but by stepping into a no-man's land where anything could and might happen.

It was just a kiss, she told herself firmly. And

yet if the baby monitor hadn't interrupted them, what then?

Short answer: nothing good.

Her skin twitched as her brain silently offered up a slideshow of herself and Ragnar, their naked bodies a perfect fit as they moved together, breath quickening in a shuddering climax.

Okay, that was a lie.

Sex with Ragnar would be fierce and tender and utterly unforgettable, but that was exactly why she should never have kissed him.

Her heart began beating a little faster. It was tempting to blame her behaviour on tiredness, or the stress of the last few days—to argue that the simmering anger between them had blurred into another kind of intense emotion and so struck a different kind of spark.

And, yes, some of those arguments were plausible, and others were true, but none of them was the reason she had kissed him. That was much more simple.

He had been standing in front of her, close enough that she could feel the heat coming off his skin, close enough that his gaze had made her think of choices, and possibilities, and a never-forgotten night of peerless pleasure.

In other words, she had kissed him because she'd wanted to.

But then he had kissed her back, his mouth parting hers, pressing her closer, until their bodies had been seamless, until she had been frantic and twisting in his arms—

Her face felt hot, the skin suddenly too tight across her cheekbones. She knew she should regret what had happened, and yet she couldn't—not quite. But that didn't mean it was going to happen again.

Clearly she and Ragnar had 'chemistry'. It seemed like such a boring word for the astonishing intensity of their attraction, for the ceaseless craving that made her breathing change pace. But, after struggling even to be civil to one another, they had finally achieved a fragile symbiosis based on what was best for Sóley. Having sex was only going to put that in jeopardy. Whatever her body might want to believe.

Sex was never simple.

Her daughter was proof of that.

She and Ragnar had used logic and mathematical certainty to select one another, on the basis that they both wanted the same thing, only that certainly hadn't included having a baby together.

But, even without putting Sóley into the equation, she knew from her own limited and un-remarkable experience that for most people, most of the time, sex was more than just bodies. There was always some kind of emotional response—regret, hope, doubt, excitement—and that response was often complex and confusingly contradictory.

Right now she didn't need any more confusion in her life, and she was going to have to find a way to express that to Ragnar.

She swore silently, and Sóley looked up at her, her eyes widening in confusion as though she had actually heard and understood the word.

'Let's go and get your lunch,' she said, and quickly, guiltily, swung her daughter up into the air and held her close, burying her face in her daughter's neck until the soft pressure of Ragnar's mouth was just a dull memory.

For the moment anyway. But she was going to have face him sooner or later.

She turned towards the house—and froze.

Ragnar was walking towards her, smoothly and steadily, his blond hair shining like bronze in the sunlight. Unlike her, he wasn't wearing a coat, just a dark jumper with jeans and boots, and suddenly her breath felt hot and slippery in her throat. He was so heart-stoppingly handsome—and, in comparison to the flickering images inside her head, as solid and unwavering as a long ship.

'Hello.'

He stopped in front of her, his eyes meeting his daughter's, his face softening in a way that made her stomach crunch into a knot of pleasure and pain.

'How was the rest of your night?'

'It was fine. She didn't wake up until nearly nine.'

Should she say something now? She hesitated. Words were not her thing, but she couldn't exactly sketch or sculpt what she needed to say to him.

His blue gaze shifted to her face. 'And what about you? Did you manage to get any sleep?'

There was a small beat of silence. Then she nodded, still tongue-tied as he stared at her impassively. And then, with relief, she saw that Signy was hurrying towards them.

'I didn't realise you were out here.' The older woman's unruffled smile cut effortlessly through the awkward silence. 'Lunch is ready. Or I could feed Sóley if you and Mr Stone are talking? I'd be more than happy to,' she added as Lottie started to protest.

But it was too late. A hungry and determined Sóley was already reaching for Signy with her arms outstretched and, heart pounding, Lottie watched helplessly as her daughter disappeared into the house.

She had no excuse now not to say something.

But before she could open her mouth he said abruptly, 'Would you like to come and have a look at the horses with me? They're out in the paddock. I thought maybe—' He frowned and stopped speaking mid-sentence, as though he'd said more than he'd intended.

She hesitated. Yesterday she would definitely have made up some excuse and refused, but today it was easier to nod and say, 'Thank you, that would be lovely.'

The horses were beautiful, and incredibly friendly. They were all different sizes and colours, from piebald through to palomino, and their coats were thick and shaggy like reindeer fur. Peeling off her gloves, she leaned over the wooden fence to touch their velvety faces. As a beautiful chestnut put his face forward for her to rub, she realised that she was enjoying herself.

Her stomach tightened. So maybe she didn't need to talk to him after all.

Here, in the bright sunlight, with the crisp air

on her skin, their kiss felt distant and dream-like. Perhaps if they stood here for long enough the brilliant blue sky might part like the sea and swallow up the memory of it entirely.

'Do you ride?'

His voice jogged her thoughts and, glancing up, she instantly realised the stupidity of that notion.

It was nearly two years since she and Ragnar had slept together and yet she could still remember every second. And not just his hard-muscled body or the careless beauty of his face. He had an aura, a disruptive, sensual energy beneath his stillness, and it separated him from every other man she'd ever met. And right now that aura was pinning her to the frozen ground and making her limbs flood with heat.

She nodded. 'I used to. When I was younger we lived in a converted farm building and the farmer's wife had horses. She let me and Lucas ride them in exchange for mucking them out.'

She felt his gaze on her profile and, looking over, found that he was staring at her intently.

'And now?'

She shrugged. 'I don't really have the time.'

His expression shifted infinitesimally, in a way

that she couldn't pinpoint—a kind of tensing in anger, but not quite.

'But you'd like to?'

As she nodded, he seemed to relax a little.

'I'll make it happen,' he said softly.

'Thank you,' she said. 'And thank you for yesterday…well, I mean this morning. For listening to me. I'm sorry to throw all that drama at you.'

'Drama?' He seemed amused or maybe surprised by her choice of word. 'You were very dignified—not dramatic at all. And I'm sorry that I made you feel excluded. Truly it wasn't and isn't my intention to push you out of Sóley's life.'

'I know. I understand that now.'

She glanced past him. There was nobody around. If she waited until they went back into the house she might have to seek out another private moment, and the thought of being alone with him inside was the spur she needed to speak.

'About what happened after we talked…'

She looked up, jolted by hearing the words she had been about to say come out of his mouth.

'You mean when I…?' She hesitated.

He gazed at her steadily. 'I mean when we kissed.'

For a second her vision blurred. It felt significant, him choosing those particular words, for he could have made it sound like her sole responsibility. Instead he was admitting his own desire had played a part.

'I thought you might want to pretend it hadn't happened,' she said.

There was a small silence, and then he shook his head. 'I don't want to do that—and even if I did I'm not sure that I could.'

His gaze fixed on her face and she felt her blood thicken and slow at the hunger in his eyes...a hunger that seemed to reach through the layers of her padded jacket so that she could feel heat spiralling up inside her.

'I know I haven't given you much reason to trust me, but trust me on this: I wanted to kiss you every bit as much you wanted to kiss me. I was just waiting for permission.' He gave her a small, taut smile. 'Look, Lottie, there's something I need to say to you. I want you to know how sorry I am for lying to you the night we met. I hope that maybe one day you'll believe that's not who I am.'

She stared at him in silence, processing his statement. He made it sound as though he'd acted out of character—but then why had he lied to her?

It was on the tip of her tongue to ask, but what

had happened early this morning had to take precedence over the past. 'Why are you telling me this now?' she asked.

'I want us to be honest with one another,' he said simply. 'About what happened and why.'

'I don't know why it happened.' She paused. He had been open with her, so he deserved honesty in return. 'Or maybe I do...' Her face tightened. 'I know it's been twenty months since we—'

There was a small silence.

'I thought you might have forgotten,' he said quietly.

She wanted to laugh. Forget him? Forget that night? 'No, I didn't forget you, Ragnar. I can't.'

'You mean Sóley—?'

The sun was in her eyes, making his face unreadable. But she hadn't been talking about her daughter, she thought with a mix of shame and panic. She had been talking about *him*, and about how he had made her feel, and the soft, urgency of his mouth, and her own quickening gasp as she arched against him.

'There hasn't been a day when I haven't thought about you,' he said.

Looking up at him, she let her gaze search his face and, seeing the heat in his eyes, she nodded, acknowledging the truth of his words and the fact that they were true for her too.

His hand came up and she breathed in sharply as his fingers traced the curve of her cheekbone. Without knowing it was what she wanted to do, or that she was going to do it, she rubbed her face against his hand.

'I thought it would pass,' he said simply.

She stared at him, hypnotised by the ache in his voice—an ache she shared. 'Me too.' With an effort she slid her head away from his hand. 'And it will… But in the meantime I don't think acting on it would be—' She stopped.

'A good idea?' he finished for her.

'It would be a very bad idea,' she agreed.

She could hardly believe she was talking to him like this, but what were the alternatives? To pretend that it was a figment of their imaginations? To listen to their libidos?

Of course she could see the appeal of both—but, while she didn't know the limits of the man standing beside her, she knew her own limits, and there was no way she could play happy families with Ragnar and have no-strings sex with him at the same time.

'We're here to be parents and I think we should concentrate on that,' she said.

'I'm glad we're on the same page,' he said quietly.

Her fingers tightened against the fence and she winced as something small and sharp dug into her skin. It was just a splinter, but it stung more than it should, and she welcomed the pain—for it gave her something to focus on other than the hollowed-out feeling in her stomach. But however much it hurt, she knew her regret at stopping things before they got started would be inconsequential compared to the fallout from a self-indulgent affair.

Straightening up, she met his gaze. 'I think we should probably get some lunch.'

'Then let's go and see what Signy has cooked for us,' he said slowly.

Lunch was a beautiful fish soup with fresh sourdough bread and the most delicious butter she had ever eaten.

After lunch, Sóley almost fell asleep in her highchair. Transferring her smoothly into his arms, Ragnar took her upstairs to bed.

Lottie watched him go. It was getting easier to let him be involved now, and it was also a relief to have a few minutes without her body being so intensely aware of exactly where he was in relation to her.

She glanced around the empty kitchen, and then wandered into the huge living space. It was a beautifully proportioned room, and the light was truly incredible. As it shifted in depth and colour it was like a kind of ever-changing art installation that perfectly complemented the striking mobile spinning and shifting in the invisible air currents.

Her pulse twitched. Mobiles were supposed to be calming, and yet she felt anything but calm.

Restlessly she moved around the room. Ragnar's taste was minimalist. Everything was pared back to its essence, each piece selected on the basis that its beauty equalled its functionality.

Surprisingly, given its stark beauty, it was still a comfortable, welcoming space—perhaps because it so clearly embodied the personality of its owner. She glanced over to the amazing rotating suspended fireplace. The room certainly didn't feel cold. She could feel the heat from the fire seeping into her blood.

Collapsing onto one of the huge leather sofas, she leaned back against the cushions and gazed upwards—straight into Ragnar's blue eyes.

'Are you tired?'

He dropped down beside her, and instantly his nearness made her breathe out of time.

'A little bit.'

The light from the fire was playing off his face and for a moment she stared at him in silence, transfixed by the shifting shadows. And then her pulse tripped over itself as he put his hand on her shoulder and pressed down lightly.

'You're tense here…'

Was she? She didn't feel tense. In fact her body felt as though it was melting.

Pull away, she told herself. *Move.*

But her limbs wouldn't respond. Instead—and completely unforgivably, given what she'd said to him at the stables—she could feel herself wanting to arch against him like a cat.

'You need to relax…'

His voice vibrated through her shoulder blade and a prickling heat spread over her skin.

'Have a bit of down-time. Maybe unwind in the pool. We could take a dip after dinner.'

Her head was spinning. There were so many dangerous words in that sentence. *Relax, unwind, pool, dip, after dinner…* And yet the idea of a relaxing swim in a hot pool was so tempting. Her eyes roamed briefly around the exquisite room. Really, when was she ever going to get a chance to live like this again?

'That sounds lovely.'

'You won't regret it.' His gaze met hers. 'In fact, your body might even thank you.'

There was no moon but it was a cloudless night and, staring up through the glass ceiling of the pool house, Ragnar allowed himself a moment to tick off the constellations in the dark sky before wading into the steam-covered water.

He breathed out slowly. It was like slipping into liquid velvet. It was incredibly warm—blood-hot, in fact—and as he lowered himself down he felt his body grow heavy with a languid, almost boneless weight.

On any other night he would have simply floated on his back and watched the stars. Now, though, he moved slowly through the water, his narrowed gaze tracking the progress of the woman making her way along the edge of the pool like a nervous gazelle at a watering hole.

His heartbeat accelerated as she slipped off the thick towelling robe and dropped it onto one of the fur-covered loungers at the side of the pool. Underneath she was wearing a caramel-coloured swimsuit, a shade darker than her eyes, which hugged her body in a way that was completely understandable.

Watching her step down into the pool, he mentally thanked Signy for reminding him to suggest that she bring one.

As the water closed over her shoulders he felt a sharp twinge of regret that no amount of geothermal heat was going to fix but, ignoring his quickening pulse, he swam towards her.

'How does it feel?'

'It feels wonderful.' Her gaze followed the steam rising up from the water. 'And a bit crazy.'

'Why crazy?' He swam a little closer, drawn in by the surprise and excitement in her face.

'I don't know—it just seems mad for there to be snow everywhere and yet the water in here's so hot.'

'Well, it is the land of fire and ice.'

'The land of fire and ice?'

She repeated his words slowly and, feeling his body respond to the eagerness in her voice, he cursed himself silently. If anything was crazy it was his suggestion that he and Lottie take a dip together beneath the stars. But of course he'd been slowly going crazy for days, his feverish brain torturing his body with images of a naked, gloriously uninhibited Lottie.

They swam slowly in silence. He usually swam alone, and when he was away from Iceland he craved his solitary moments in the pool, but with

Lottie beside him he felt an entirely different kind of craving, and he was shocked by how badly he wanted to give into it.

His stomach clenched. It made no sense after what he'd said earlier, and what she'd said, and yet it was there—a need, a hunger, a heat that had nothing to with any geothermal activity.

'Do you use the pool a lot?' she asked softly.

He nodded. 'Usually once a day. Sometimes twice. During the day you can see the sky reflected in the water and it's like you're swimming among the clouds.'

She turned towards him, her eyes wide and unguarded, and he felt something squeeze in his chest at the surprise he saw there.

'I didn't have you down as a poet,' she said.

For a moment, he was captivated by the softness in her voice, and then he felt an almost vertiginous rush of panic.

Glancing upwards, he felt his body loosen with relief. 'I know my limits. If you want real poetry, you just need to look up.'

She gasped. Above them, the sky seemed to be melting. Colour was suffusing the darkness, lighting up the night, and swathes of green and amber and amethyst were swirling and shifting like oil on water.

It was the Aurora Borealis—the Northern Lights—but Ragnar barely noticed the dazzling display. He was too busy watching Lottie.

He breathed out unsteadily. His body was alive with need, worse than before, and his heart hammered in his ears so that thinking was impossible. But he didn't need a conscious brain to know that he still wanted Lottie.

And then, just like that, the show was over.

'We should go in,' he said quietly.

She nodded, following him reluctantly out of the pool. 'Did you know that was going to happen?'

He held out the robe. 'Only in that it's a clear night and it's the right time of year.'

He hardly knew what he was saying, but what he did know was that he still regretted those lies he'd told her that first night. And if he didn't tell her what he was thinking now, wasn't that just a different kind of lie? One he would regret for ever?

So tell her the truth. Be honest, like you said you wanted to be.

He met her gaze, felt his pulse stilling. His home here in Iceland was his sanctuary. A place of calm and order. If he said what he was thinking then he ran the risk of unleashing chaos and passion here.

But if he didn't, what then?

The chaos would still be there, underneath the surface, and it wasn't going anywhere.

And now, finally, he understood why. Ever since that night in the hotel room he hadn't felt whole. The panic that had led him to slip away while she slept still haunted him, and only by owning this hunger was he going to restore balance to his life.

'Earlier…when I talked about what happened… I think I was wrong. Actually, I *know* I was wrong.' He frowned. 'What I'm trying to say is this thing between us, I know it's complicated and confusing…but it's also real, and pretending it isn't would be a lie. I think you feel the same way. But if you don't, that's okay. I just need you to tell me and then I'll never—'

'I do.' She swallowed. 'I do feel the same way.'

His eyes dropped to her mouth. Had she spoken or had he just imagined it?

'Are you sure?' he said hoarsely.

'About wanting you? Yes.'

She looked away and, reaching out, he gently framed her face with his hands. 'We don't need to have all the answers, Lottie.' He was surprised to find that he meant what he said. 'We can work it out together.'

She breathed out shakily and his own breath stalled in his throat as she let the robe slide from her fingers to the floor. For a few pulsing half-seconds she stared at him in silence, and then she took his right hand from her cheek and pressed the palm against her breast.

He felt his pulse accelerate, his body hardening with a speed that almost made him black out, and then, leaning forward he kissed her. Only not in the way she'd kissed him in the kitchen. This was a raw and urgent kiss, a kiss without restraint, a kiss designed to satisfy the hunger in both of them.

'You have no idea how much I want you,' he murmured against her mouth. 'I haven't been able to get you out of my mind.'

'Me too,' she whispered. She was leaning into him so that their foreheads were touching, their warm breath mingling. 'It's like you're in my head...'

Her voice, that beautiful husky voice, made his body loosen with desire. Beneath his hand he could feel her nipple tightening through the damp fabric of her swimsuit and, breathing raggedly, he began caressing the swollen tip with his thumb, liking the way it made her arch into him and the sudden quickening of her breath.

Her hands were clutching him and tugging him closer, pulling at the waistband of his shorts, and then she pressed her hand against the hard ridge of his body and he groaned.

'Let's go upstairs—' He was fighting to get the words out.

'No.' Her voice was husky with need.

He tried to protest, but it turned into another groan as her fingers slid beneath the waistband. Recognising defeat, he picked her up and dropped her onto the nearest lounger. As she sprawled backwards on the fur he took a step away and, keeping his eyes trained on her face, he slid down his shorts.

CHAPTER SEVEN

HIS HEART WAS slamming against his ribs like a door in a gale.

Had any woman ever looked sexier? She was sprawled against the fur, her eyes wide and feverish, her damp hair spilling over her shoulders. Like the ice in spring, he felt his blood start to melt as his gaze dropped lower. The wet fabric of her swimsuit looked so much like melted caramel all he could think about was how it would feel to lick it off the curves of her body.

It was suddenly difficult to swallow past the hunger swelling in his throat, and without even really knowing that he was doing so he moved swiftly to join her.

Her skin was hot to touch, and dotted with drops of water like tiny transparent pearls. Leaning forward, he touched the one closest with the tip of his tongue and then, keeping his eyes fixed on her face, he traced a path to the next one, and the next, feeling her tremble at his touch.

'Ragnar…'

She murmured his name, and it was the sweetest sound he'd ever heard. He stretched out over her and kissed her hungrily. She cupped his face with her hands and kissed him back. They broke apart to catch their breath, and then without a word he reached out and slid first one and then the other strap away from her shoulders, peeling the damp costume away from her body until she was naked.

He breathed out unsteadily, staying his hunger to admire her high, firm breasts and slightly rounded stomach. 'You're so beautiful,' he whispered and, lowering his face, he ran his tongue over her nipples, tasting the salt from the water as she arched upwards, pressing against him, offering herself to the heat of his mouth.

And then she was jerking free, her eyes dark and fierce, and he breathed in sharply as she reached for him, wrapping her fingers around his hard length. His hand gripped hers but she batted him away, bending over him to brush her lips against him. And then she was taking him into her mouth and he was groaning, his fingers grasping her hair, his body gripped by a pleasure so intense it was almost painful.

He was fiercely aroused, his body tight to the

point of breaking. The feel of her mouth was turning him inside out. He was so close, *too close*—

Clenching his teeth, wanting, needing to be inside her, he pulled away, moving with panicky suspended hunger to fit his body against hers.

'Ragnar…'

Her fingernails dug into his back, but it was the urgency in her voice that cut through his heartbeat.

'I'm not protected.'

Not protected.

He stared down at her, blood roaring in his ears. His preoccupied overheated body was making it hard to think clearly and her words were bouncing off his dazed brain like hailstones on a roof.

And then he swore silently—not just at the implied consequences of that statement, but at his own near-adolescent loss of control. Had he really been so caught up in the moment that he'd forgotten all about contraception?

Catching sight of her small set face, he put his shock and shame to one side and, blanking out the relentless ache in his groin, captured her face between her hands and kissed her gently. 'It's okay…we don't have to—'

He breathed out against her cheek, fighting to contain the desperation in his voice. He would rather wait than put her under pressure.

Her fingers tightened against his arms. 'I want to, only I don't have any condoms.'

'It's okay,' he said again. 'I don't either—well, not here, anyway.'

He didn't want her to think that he wasn't careful, and nor did he want it to look as if he'd made assumptions about what would happen here tonight.

She bit her lip. 'There hasn't really been anyone since… That's why I'm not…why I haven't…'

He didn't know why but her words made a warm ripple of relief spread over his skin, and without meaning to, he said softly, 'There hasn't been anyone for me either.'

Her eyes widened. He wasn't sure if she believed him. Hearing it out loud, he found it difficult to believe too, but it was true. After what had happened with Lottie he'd buried himself in work, too unnerved by the failure of his mathematical certainties to test them again in person.

She breathed out unsteadily. 'We should probably go inside.'

The prospect of returning to his room alone

made his body tense—with hunger, not misery—but he managed to nod. 'Yes, we should.'

He felt her lean into him, and hesitate, and then she said shakily, 'My room or yours?'

The air swelled around them, swallowing up her question and retreating. He stared down at her in confusion. 'I don't— We don't— I'm not—'

Her wide-eyed, panicky gaze met his. 'Have you changed your mind?'

Hope fought with fear, and he gripped her tightly. 'You know I haven't. I can't. There's nothing inside my head except you.'

He heard her slow intake of breath.

'My room then,' she said quickly, and this time his relief was swift and sharp.

They dressed and he led her back into the house, moving purposefully through the darkness. Her heart was beating out of time and too fast, the aftershocks of their feverish almost-coupling mingling with a leaping panic. She was scared of leaving the starlit heat of the pool house, scared that the shift in mood and pace might introduce a change of perspective.

But as they walked upstairs she felt his hand tighten, and then he was pulling her against him, his mouth blindly seeking hers, kissing her with such blazing urgency that she forgot where she was and who she was, and there was nothing but the darkness and their staccato breathing and the insistent pressure of his mouth.

They made it to her bedroom—just. She had left the curtains open and, using the light from the pool house, they stripped again and kissed their way to the bed.

And then any fears she'd had about coming upstairs were forgotten as he raised her hips and gently nudged her legs apart. She felt his breath on her skin, and then her own breath seemed to stick in her throat as his tongue found the pulse between her thighs and began to move with slow, sure precision.

A moan of pleasure rose to her lips and her eyes slipped backwards. And then she was clasping his head, pushing him deeper, then pulling back, wanting more, but not wanting it to end. She felt weightless and her head was spinning. Heat was spilling over her skin in waves, each one faster and stronger than the last, so that her whole body was vibrating. And then she was tensing, pressing against his quickening tongue, her hands jerking through his hair.

She felt him move up the bed and then his

mouth was on hers, pushing and parting her lips, probing her mouth and then dropping to lick her throat, her collarbone, her nipples. Her breath caught in her throat. He felt solid, harder and bigger than before. Was this how it worked? It had been so long she couldn't remember.

'It's okay,' he whispered, his lips brushing her mouth, his fingers sliding inside her, oscillating back and forth until her skin was tightening, her body melting against him.

She found her voice. 'Do you have the—?'

'Are you sure?' He spoke through gritted teeth and she knew he was holding himself in check.

'Yes, I'm sure.'

He rolled off the bed and moved swiftly to the door. Watching him leave, she curled her fingers into the sheet. His absence felt like an actual physical loss—like the sun dropping behind cloud—but suddenly he was back, tearing open the packet and rolling on the condom with smooth, precise care, then sliding back down beside her.

He pulled her against him, and as his mouth found hers she pulled him closer still, her hands pressing against his back, reaching down to hold his hips, and then she was guiding him into her body.

His eyes were rapt and unblinking in the half-light, his face taut with concentration and a need that mirrored her own as he moved against her in time to her accelerating heartbeat. And then she felt him tense, and he was thrusting into her, filling her completely, his groan mingling with her soft cry as her muscles tightened sharply around his hard, convulsing body.

He collapsed beside her, pressing his face into the curve of her collarbone, and she clung to him weakly. They were both breathing raggedly, their bodies slick with sweat, but she wanted to lie there for ever. Finally, though, he shifted his weight and pulled out of her. For the briefest half-second she thought he'd pull away completely. Instead, though, he drew her back against him.

'I was careful…'

'I know,' she whispered, surprised but grateful that he had understood her nervousness about contraception.

His arm curved around her back, and he kept it there as his breathing slowed.

And that was how they must have fallen asleep.

She wasn't sure what woke her, but even before her eyes were properly open she was aware of the solid warmth of his body beside hers and her body's instant and unqualified response to it. Her heartbeat slowed. For a moment she kept her eyes shut. She just couldn't bring herself to open them, for to do so would mean having to return to reality, to clothes, and to being composed and civilised. She wanted to stay here in his arms for ever—to be the woman she had become in his arms.

Her body felt loose and languid, and yet she had never felt more alive, more at one with herself and the world and her place in it. If only she could freeze time...just until she was ready.

She shivered. But ready for what?

There was only one way to find out.

Opening her eyes, she felt her pulse scamper forward. Ragnar was watching her, his gaze more grey than blue in the predawn half-light.

'Morning,' he said softly.

Her eyes had adjusted to the light now, and she gazed up at him, trying to read his expression. Not once during the night had she felt that he was regretting their decision, and nor did she feel any regret for what they'd done. But cocooned in darkness, sheltering in one another's arms, it had been easy to feel as if they were in their own little world, outside of time and answerable to no one.

'What time is it?' she asked quietly.

'About six.' He hesitated, his face stilling as though he was working something through in his head. 'Sorry, did I wake you?'

Shaking her head, she met his gaze. 'No, I'm nearly always awake by six.' She gave him a small, swift smile. 'Sóley doesn't really do lie-ins yet.'

There were three beats of silence.

Her right leg was curled over his left, and she could feel the prickle of his hair against her skin, but what did this physical closeness really mean?

Inside her head, a nervous round of questions began firing off like party poppers. What was he thinking? Had the night changed things for him as it had for her?

The questions, or maybe the thought of his possible answers, made her stomach tighten.

Was having sex really that big a deal?

She felt her face grow hot at the stupidity of her words. Yes, it was—and not because there had been nobody since that first time with Ragnar. Last night had been about more than satisfying her hunger. It had felt like an admission of something other than sex.

Her heart began to pound. Or was she just doing what she'd done with Alistair? Building castles in the air? Letting her imagination play fast and loose with the facts?

'About last night—'

They both spoke at the same time.

Her chest tightened as his eyes lifted to her face. 'You think it was a mistake?' he said.

'Do you?' she prompted. Her heart was beating so loudly now she felt sure that it must have moved from her chest into her head.

He stared at her for what felt like half a lifetime and then he shook his head. 'No, I don't.'

'I don't either.' She spoke quickly, relief making her words run into one another like a runaway train's coaches hitting the buffers.

There was another beat of silence, and then he reached out and pulled her close, kissed her with the same urgency he had in the darkness. Her heart was still pounding, but with his lips on hers the tightness in her chest began to ease.

Finally, he raised his mouth and rubbed his face against hers, so that she could feel his warm breath on her skin. 'So, what happens next?'

It felt strange, hearing her own words come out of his mouth, for asking him that question had been a defining moment in her life. It was as if they had come full circle.

Only back then everything had been possible. Standing outside the restaurant, pressed up against the heat of his body and with his blue gaze resting on her face, she had felt as though they had a limitless number of futures, some too distant to fully imagine, others too fragile to be considered seriously, but all of them had been out there.

Now, though, too much reality had come between them—good and bad—for her to feel like that.

But what was she feeling? Did she even know?

Closing her mind to the confusion of her thoughts, she let her eyes drift over the hard muscles of his chest and stomach, then lower to where the hair grew most thickly.

What she did know was that she didn't want to walk away just yet.

'Lottie?'

His blue gaze was searching her face, only she didn't know what to say. She was more confused than ever, but it seemed incredibly important not to offer up something less than the truth.

She looked up at him and swallowed. 'I want this. I want you.'

His eyes locked with hers. 'And I want you too. Emphatically. Completely. Shamelessly.'

His fingers traced the curve of her hipbone as

he spoke, so that suddenly she was squirming against him.

'And I don't want to turn away from this thing between us. Not yet.'

The certainty in his voice was captivating, and she stared at him spellbound.

'Let's give ourselves these three weeks.'

He was spelling it out for her, making it simple for both of them in a way that had been beyond her, and she was grateful that one of them had managed to put it into words.

'And afterwards you'll still be Sóley's mother and I'll still be her father—just like we agreed.'

'So we just carry on as we are?' she said slowly.

He nodded. 'Until we stop.'

His blue eyes were clear and calm and irresistible. Breathing in his warm scent, she nodded slowly, and as she leaned into him they began to taste one another all over again.

'How do you feel about taking the horses out after lunch? I'd like to show you the estate while you're here.'

Keeping his eyes fixed on Lottie's face, Ragnar leaned forward and refilled her water glass. They were having lunch alone today. Sóley had already eaten and gone upstairs for her nap, and they were eating in the dining area.

It was a glorious room, with a glorious view, and normally he simply sat back and enjoyed the contrast between the restrained luxury of the interior and the stark wilderness outside the glass. Today, though, his gaze kept returning to the woman sitting opposite him.

It was easier between them now. She was still quieter than any woman he'd ever met—certainly quieter than any in his family—but her quietness no longer felt like a show of defiance. Now that he wasn't so on edge himself, he realised that if she was quiet it was because she was concentrating, really listening to what he said.

And not just listening. When her gaze was on his face it felt as if her soft brown eyes were reaching inside him.

'What about Sóley?'

He stared at her blankly. Caught in the honey-eyed trap of her eyes, he'd lost track of the conversation.

With an effort, he refocused his thoughts. 'We'll only be out for an hour or so at the most before we lose the light, and Signy is desperate to spend some time with her.' Sensing her uncertainty, he changed tack. 'But if Sóley isn't happy to be left then we won't go, obviously.'

'I'd really like to see the estate, and I'd love to go riding.' She glanced longingly through the glass, and then her face creased. 'But I don't have any jodhpurs or boots or a helmet.'

'That won't be a problem. When you said you liked to ride I had one of my people pick up everything you need.'

She frowned. 'But how did you know my size?'

He held her gaze, feeling his body respond in about fifty different ways to her words. 'I know how you fit against me, so I just scaled down.' His eyes flickered over the high curve of her breasts. 'With a few adjustments.'

Signy chose that moment to come and check their plates and find out if they wanted coffee or tea, and he took the opportunity to make sure she was happy to look after Sóley.

When they were finally alone, he looked back across the table at Lottie. The curve of her cheekbones was still pink and, watching her fingers slide up the stem of the glass, he felt his body stiffen to granite hardness. It was all too easy to remember her hand moving in just such a way but for a very different purpose.

Picking up his own glass, he drank some water.

It was refreshingly chilled, but unfortunately its cooling effects ended at his stomach and didn't extend to his blood. He was starting to think that where Lottie was concerned nothing was going to change the way his body felt about her.

Earlier, as her hot skin had fused with his, desire as raw and potent as moonshine had driven all conscious thoughts and most unconscious ones from his head. He'd never been so perfectly out of control in his life, and Lottie's unrestrained, passionate response had left him craving more.

Only, was that *all* he was craving?

His heartbeat accelerated.

At any other time in his life, with any other woman, his answer would have been an unequivocal yes. But, remembering how he had felt when finally he'd forced himself to leave her bed that morning, he felt his chest grow tight.

Whatever he had said to Lottie, did he really believe that they could just stop and go back to their own lives at the end of three weeks? More importantly, did he want them to?

He tensed. The answer to that was an unequivocal no. And it wasn't just sex. Living with Lottie and Sóley felt right; they were a family now.

And that was great—except he already had

a family, and the idea of introducing one to the other was just not something he could handle right now.

Maybe not ever...

Thirty minutes later Ragnar zipped up his jacket and gazed at the sky. The sun was rising at a shallower angle every day, and today it was barely visible behind a low, bleached grey bank of cloud, but at least it wasn't raining or snowing.

There were any number of possible routes he could have chosen for today's ride, but he'd said that he wanted Lottie to see the estate, and that meant heading up the hillside.

He might have made a different decision if Lottie had been a less experienced rider but, although it was true that she was a little rigid at the start, once she'd relaxed on Orvar, the beautiful chestnut gelding he'd chosen for her, he could see that she had perfect balance and an easy, open riding style.

Turning his own horse—a bay mare called Camille—away from the jagged iced-up edge of a stream, he moved steadily with her towards the ridge, letting the horses choose the pace, trusting them to pick their way across the uneven ground.

Feeling his phone vibrate inside his jacket, he gritted his teeth. The ongoing saga between his mother and half-sister had now sucked in his ex-stepfather Nathan and his other half-sister Freya, and he was desperate to find a resolution.

Glancing over at the expression of unguarded sweetness on Lottie's face, he felt his heart beat faster. Right now, they could wait.

'How are you doing?' he asked.

'Fine.' She smiled shyly. 'I think that's more down to Orvar than me. I mean, he's a strong horse, but I just have to switch my weight a little and he does exactly what I want. He's so quick to react, so responsive.'

He turned to look across at her, a pulse beating down his spine. 'Not with everyone. He is a strong horse, but you're not fighting his strength. Your hands are gentle, and that's why he's not pulling.' His eyes locked with hers. 'Like a lot of powerful males, he just needs the right handling. I think he's okay with you being the boss.'

He watched her fingers curl against the reins.

'Probably because he knows it's only going to be a short ride,' she said quietly.

His phone vibrated again and, watching the curiosity in her eyes, he realised that he would have to answer it after all.

'Sorry. I'm going to have to take this,' he said and, unzipping his jacket, he pulled out his phone.

* * *

Watching Ragnar edge his horse away, Lottie breathed out unsteadily.

She had thought that getting away from the house and out into the cool air would be a good idea. Obviously it was going to be difficult to make sense of how she was feeling in Ragnar's home, and with Ragnar himself so distractingly close.

Mounting Orvar, it had been easy to persuade herself that the way she was feeling was normal for someone who had just had sex after nearly two years of celibacy. Not just take-it-or-leave-it sex, either. Ragnar made her head swim. And, after thinking about it for so long, it was only natural that she was going to have some kind of emotional response to his relationship with Sóley.

But now, out here in the pale grey light, with the cool wind in her face, they weren't having sex, and Sóley was back at the house, and yet the feeling of her world turning upside down persisted.

She glanced over to where Ragnar was talking. It was impossible not to catch occasional snippets of his conversation and it was clear that he was comforting someone—someone female.

'Okay, I will talk to Nathan, but you have to apologise. Because she's our mother—'

Her pulse jumped a beat.

Not just someone—his sister.

Her head was spinning. So was this Nathan his brother?

Shifting against the saddle, she breathed out slowly. She didn't even know he *had* a sister or a brother—in fact, given the lack of any photos around the house and his reclusive lifestyle, she'd assumed he didn't have a family. But clearly he did, and clearly he cared about them—a lot. So why hadn't he said anything about them before?

Her pulse jumped again. Probably because he hadn't trusted her any more than she had trusted him.

It was a disconcerting thought, but before she could pursue all its implications she realised that Ragnar had hung up and was riding towards her.

'Sorry about that.'

His face was unreadable, probably intentionally so, but now that she'd got past the shock of discovering he had a family she wanted to know more—for the obvious reason that Ragnar's family was also Sóley's.

'Is everything okay?'

For a moment she thought he wasn't going to

answer her, and then he stared past her, his eyes fixed on the horizon. 'It will be.'

She took a breath. 'So was that your sister?'

His hesitation was so brief she might not have noticed it but for the slight tensing along his jaw.

'Yes—Marta.'

Holding her breath, she waited.

Finally, he said stiffly, 'She's had a row with our mother. It's nothing really… It's just my mother has rules and Marta pushes back. But it'll blow over—it always does.'

She nodded slowly. 'At least she can call you if she needs someone to talk to.'

'Yes, I suppose she can.' He nudged Camille forward. 'Come on, it's not far now.'

And that was that.

They reached the top of the ridge ten minutes later.

Pulling up her horse, she stopped and stared. It was an incredible view.

In the distance, she could just see the blue glint of a glacier. Closer than that, snow-covered fields bumped up against twisting towers of haphazard jagged rocks in every shade of grey and silver, and then, nearer still, twin one-hundred-foot waterfalls cascaded down black basalt cliffs.

'Can we get closer?' she asked.

He nodded. 'We can walk underneath them, if you want.'

It took them another fifteen minutes to reach the waterfalls. They left the horses by the edge of a small geothermal pool. Steam from the water had melted the ice, revealing some surprisingly green grass, and both horses instantly lowered their heads and began to graze.

Behind the falls the noise of the water hitting the rock was ear-splittingly loud, and after a moment of neck-tilting admiration they moved far enough away that they could speak without having to shout.

She frowned. 'I should have brought my camera.'

'Here.' He handed her his phone. 'Use this.'

'Thank you.'

Clambering up onto a rock, she took her time to frame the picture, conscious of his gaze and of the questions building up inside her head.

'So, how many siblings do you have?' she asked as she slithered off the rock.

She felt him tense at her question. Then, 'Seven.'

'Seven!'

She turned towards him, not bothering to hide

her surprise. As a child she'd desperately wanted to be part of a big family—mainly because she hadn't always felt as if she belonged in her small one—and she could feel herself falling for a different version of the same fantasy now.

'Wow, you're so lucky. And do they all live in Iceland?'

'Sometimes.' A muscle ticked in his jaw.

'So why did you choose to live out here miles from anyone?'

He shrugged. 'Why does anyone choose to live anywhere?'

Ragnar let out an uneven breath. His chest felt as though a band of steel was wrapped around it, getting tighter and tighter.

He always found it stressful talking about his family, but here, now, with Lottie, and with that stupid conversation about giving themselves three weeks still ringing in his ears, he felt as though he might fly into a thousand pieces.

But it was ridiculous to feel that way. She was only asking him what any normal person would ask, so why was he reacting as if she was conducting an inquisition?

His shoulders tensed. He was making such a

mess of this. Why didn't he just tell her what he was thinking? Why didn't he just say that he'd got it wrong? That, waking this morning—no, even before that, holding her last night—he'd felt something shift inside him, so that now he didn't want her to disappear from his life at the end of three weeks.

Shoving his hands into his pockets, he felt his knuckles bump into his phone and he felt the tension in his shoulders spread to his spine.

What was he supposed to do?

He only knew one way of managing his life, and that was to keep all the different parts separate—and up until now it had worked just fine. His family had nothing to do with his business, and his private life was private. But Lottie and Sóley would have to meet his family, and then what?

His brain felt as though it might explode. He didn't know the answer to that. But it was impossible to see the hurt expression on Lottie's face and not know that he was the reason for it. And he didn't like how that made him feel. Or the fact that she'd had exactly the same expression when she'd been talking about her useless father.

She deserved to know the truth, or at least an

edited version of the truth, but he couldn't explain the messy, melodramatic dynamic of his family out here on this beautiful, tranquil day. And nor did he want to expose her to the mesmerising pull of their drama just yet. He knew what would happen if he did. Lottie and Sóley would be absorbed into the chaos and he couldn't bear for that to happen.

Only he wanted to give her something.

He couldn't change the past, or give her the father she deserved. But he could give her a part of himself he'd never shared with anyone else.

'My mother's family had a house not far from here. We used to come every holiday and one summer, when I was about eight, I met a boy about my age—Daniel. He was with his father, fishing in the lake over there.'

It had been the holiday before his parents had divorced—six months before his father had found out about his mother's affair—and the rows had been volcanic in their scope and ferocity, and seemingly endless in those long days of summer.

'They taught me how to fish and I caught a salmon—my first.' He grinned at the memory.

'Then we went back to their house and cooked it. It was the best meal I'd ever eaten.'

And not just because of the freshness of the fish or the fact that he'd caught it. Daniel's house had been small and simply decorated, but his parents had been so calm and patient, and it had been so relaxing he'd actually fallen asleep.

'And that's why you like coming here?'

She looked confused, and something in her soft brown gaze made him reach out and pull her against him. He could see how his words would make no sense to her, but there was no way to recreate his childish astonishment at discovering there was another way to be a family—a way without drama.

He couldn't reveal how, sitting in that quiet, ordinary little house, he'd made up his mind to live his life in just such a way, and how living that kind life meant never giving in to the unnamed feeling in his chest.

Already he'd let her get too close—closer than he should. He'd felt her happiness and her pain as his own, and he couldn't let that keep happening. He couldn't risk being swamped by emotions he couldn't handle and didn't want to feel. He needed to keep his feelings under wraps and then everything would be fine.

And if that was what he had to do to keep Lottie and Sóley in his life then that was what he would do.

What other choice did he have?

CHAPTER EIGHT

LEANING FORWARD OVER the banister, Lottie felt her heart jump guiltily against her ribs. Sóley had decided to pull her socks off and push them into her breakfast cereal, and she'd only come upstairs to grab a clean pair for her. But as she'd been walking back along the galleried landing she'd heard an irresistible squeal of laughter, and then a deeper, definitely male laugh, and she'd had to flatten her body into the cool brickwork to even out her breathing.

Now she was smiling. In the living area below, Ragnar was playing hide and seek with their daughter, and she watched, transfixed, her smile widening, as he allowed himself to be found, much to Sóley's giggling, appreciative amusement.

A week ago she would have found it impossible to enjoy this moment. She would have wanted to, only her fear of being pushed out would have overridden her good intentions. Now, though, she felt differently. She knew that the father-daughter bond wasn't a threat to her own relationship with Sóley.

She inched backwards, concealing herself in the shadows, feeling a knot of nervous uncertainty tightening beneath her diaphragm.

She felt differently about other things too.

Instead of feeling as if she was trapped in a villain's lair, out in the wilderness, she felt almost as much at home as she did in Suffolk. And, rather than counting down the days until she could leave, she was trying to stretch out every minute.

Mostly, though, she felt differently about Ragnar.

Oh, she could remember her resentment and her scepticism, but they seemed to have broken up and melted away like spring ice on a lake.

She thought back to their conversation the morning after that first time they'd yielded to the burning, incessant pull of their desire. It had been a little nerve-racking, waking in *his* arms in *her* bed. She'd had no idea of what to expect, knowing only that she didn't regret what had happened.

But then they'd talked—or rather he'd talked— and she'd agreed with him that she didn't want it to be just that one night and that they should give themselves these three weeks.

Only down by the waterfalls she'd started to realise that wasn't what she wanted either—or at least not *all* she wanted.

That phone call from his sister had made her want to learn more about this man who was Sóley's father, whose touch turned her inside out but about whom she knew next to nothing.

The knot in her stomach tightened. But, judging by his terse, oblique answers to her questions, and the shuttered expression on his face, he clearly didn't trust her enough to give her more than a glimpse into his life—a glimpse that had confused more than clarified her understanding of him.

But could she blame him for being reluctant to open up?

Even her decision to tell him about Sóley had been framed as much by her failed relationship with her own father as by a need to do the right thing.

She'd been so preoccupied by her fears of being pushed out that she'd relegated his feelings, and his family, to second place—to the point of never even actually asking him a single question about them.

Her stomach muscles clenched. He was clearly the polestar of his family. Marta had called again twice, and his mother once, and listening to him talk to them, patiently and calmly, she had felt both moved and almost envious that they had a permanent right to his attention, and she—

She pushed the words away, letting them be pulled into the swirling centrifuge of emotions she couldn't seem to unpick or understand.

Downstairs in the living area, Sóley was gratifyingly excited to see her. Kneeling down on the rug, she let her daughter climb into her arms.

'She missed you.'

Turning towards where Ragnar sat, slouching against one of the huge leather sofas, she felt her heart slip sideways. He was wearing a thin blue V-neck sweater a shade darker than his eyes, and a lock of blond hair was falling across his forehead. He looked calm and relaxed and incredibly sexy.

'Sorry for taking so long.'

He shifted against the sofa, stretching his leg out so that his thigh was next to hers, and instantly the heat and pressure of his body made her breathing change rhythm.

'You really don't need to keep apologising to me every time I look after her. Otherwise I'm going to have start retrospectively apologising to you for the last eleven months.'

'I just don't want to take you for granted.'

His eyes rested on her face, the blue suddenly very blue. 'How *do* you want to take me?' he said softly.

Behind the sudden insistent thud of her heart-beat she heard her phone vibrate on the sofa. It could be her mum, or Lucas, or even Georgina to say that the gallery had burned down, but she couldn't seem to make herself care enough to pick it up and find out.

'Here.' He reached across and handed her the phone. 'It might be a commission. Just because I'm on holiday it doesn't mean you have to be too.'

Thankful for being given a reason to lower her face, away from his steady stare, she glanced down at the screen as her mind nervously tried to interpret his words.

He was talking about being on holiday from his job, not commenting on their affair. Or was he?

She wanted to ask him so badly that words filled her throat and mouth. *Is this just a holiday romance? Is that why you don't want to tell me anything about your family?*

But she wasn't brave enough to find out for sure.

Glancing down at the screen, she saw that it wasn't a commission—just a message from Lucas telling her that he'd fixed the leak in the workshop and asking if she thought a swing would be a good idea for Sóley's birthday.

She laid her phone down on the rug, pushing Lucas's question to the back of her mind. It should be the biggest date in her calendar, but right now she didn't want to think about her daughter's first birthday, for that would mean planning for the future—a future in which she would no longer wake to find Ragnar's warm body beside hers or fall asleep in his arms.

'All okay?'

Blocking the hollow ache in her stomach, she looked up and nodded. 'Yes, it's just Lucas.' Afraid that he might read her thoughts, she turned towards her daughter. 'Right, you, let's get these socks—'

But before she had a chance to finish her sentence Sóley had wriggled off her lap, snatched the phone off the rug and begun crawling across the floor at great speed.

'You little monkey!' Laughing, Lottie chased after her, scooping her daughter into her arms and burying her face in her stomach until Sóley was squirming and giggling uncontrollably.

Having retrieved her phone, she lowered her still giggling daughter to the rug. She could feel Sóley straightening her legs, steadying herself as she had been doing for last few weeks, pulling impatiently against her mother's restraining hands.

'Okay—you can stand by yourself.'

For a few seconds or more her daughter swayed on the spot, finding her balance, and then she raised her arms, cooing breathlessly towards where her father was kneeling in front of the huge suspended fireplace.

Watching him toss in a couple of logs, Lottie felt her heart begin to pound.

'Ragnar...' She spoke his name softly, and as he turned towards her, her eyes met his and she smiled. 'She wants you,' she prompted.

He started to get up, but she shook her head. 'No, say her name.'

A flicker of understanding passed across his

face and he stayed crouched down, his eyes fixed on his daughter as Lottie lifted her phone.

'Sóley.'

His voice was raw-sounding, and she could tell that he was struggling to hold on to his composure.

'Sóley, come to Daddy.' He hesitated and then repeated himself in Icelandic.

Holding her breath, Lottie watched as Sóley teetered towards his outstretched hands, taking one wobbly step after another like a tiny astronaut, and then she stopped, weaving unsteadily on the rug. And as she tipped forward he caught her in his arms.

Lottie switched off her phone camera, tears burning her eyes as Ragnar got unsteadily to his feet, still holding his daughter close, pressing his face into her loose blonde curls. And then suddenly he was walking across the room and pulling her into his arms, pulling her close.

Burying her wet face against his shoulder, still clutching her phone, she breathed out unsteadily.

'Thank you,' he said softly.

Her hands gripped his sweater. 'For what?'

'Her first steps.'

She felt his emotion in her own chest. 'I'm just sorry it took me so long to let you be her father, and for being so wrapped up in my-self. I should have asked you about your family before—especially after burdening you with what happened with my father—'

His arms tightened around her. 'You didn't burden me with anything. I'm glad you told me. And, just for the record, I think your father made the biggest mistake of his life giving up the chance to know you. You're an incredible person, Lottie.'

She shook her head. 'I'm not. I've been selfish and self-absorbed.'

'And I've been overbearing and manipulative and cold-blooded.' His eyes were gleaming, but his voice was gentle.

Recognising her own words, she smiled. 'Did I say that?'

He smiled back at her—a sweet, slow smile that made her insides loosen.

'I probably deserved worse.'

Lottie laughed. 'I definitely *thought* worse.' She took a breath. 'I'll send you that video and you can share it with your family.'

Maybe her daughter's first steps might be *her* first step towards making amends.

'I've got other videos,' she added. 'I can send those too.

He was silent for a moment, and then he said, 'I'd like to see them.'

Her eyes flicked to his face. There was something different about his voice… Only before she had a chance to consider what had changed, or why, Sóley leaned forward and grabbed her shoulder, pulling all three of them into an embrace.

Her heart was suddenly thumping hard inside her chest, as she pictured the three of them in her garden in Suffolk: she and Ragnar were taking turns to push their daughter in her swing, their eyes bright, their faces flushed with the chilled air and with something less tangible that she couldn't name—

She cleared her throat. 'I was thinking… I know you're already taking time off work now, so don't worry if you can't,' she said quickly. 'But I was just wondering if you'd like to come to Suffolk for Sóley's birthday? It's not a party, or anything, but I know she'd love you to be there.' She hesitated. 'I'd love you to be there too.'

He was staring at her steadily, and she felt heat rise up over her throat and curl around her neck like a cashmere scarf.

'I'd like that very much.'

'Excuse me, Mr Stone— Oh, I'm so sorry—'

It was Signy.

Lottie felt her cheeks grow warm. She had no idea whether or not Ragnar's housekeeper had detected a change in their relationship, but she didn't want to make the older woman feel in any way uncomfortable.

'No need to apologise, Signy,' Ragnar said calmly. 'Sóley just started walking and we were celebrating.' He hesitated. 'In fact, why don't we celebrate properly? We have champagne, don't we, Signy?'

'Yes, we do, Mr Stone.'

'Good.'

Lottie watched as he gently kissed his daughter's forehead, and then the air was squeezed from her lungs as he lowered his mouth and brushed his lips against hers.

'Then let's celebrate.'

Leaning back in his chair, Ragnar stared down at his laptop, watching the cursor blink on the pitifully blank screen. On the desk beside him he had a neatly stacked pile of unread business plans and magazines. But it didn't matter how neatly they were stacked—he already knew they were definitely going to stay unread.

Two years ago, when his business had been

starting up and he'd felt as if a hosepipe filled with data was pumping non-stop into his head, he'd followed the example of other successful CEOs and taken a couple of 'think weeks' out of his schedule.

He found them incredibly productive, and now he was following the same rules as he always did. Web-browsing was forbidden, he could only check emails once a day, for no more than fifteen minutes, and he could take no business calls whatsoever. The idea was to remove all distractions from his life and allow his mind the space and freedom to reset his goals, so that when he did return to work he would hit the ground running—and in the right direction.

He glanced again at the blinking cursor.

But clearly some distractions were just way more distracting than others, he thought, his body hardening as a slow-motion replay of the morning shower he'd shared with Lottie slid unprompted into his head.

He gritted his teeth. No wonder he was finding it difficult to focus his thoughts.

Except that wasn't true. His thoughts *were* focused—only not on the future direction of his business but on the woman who had managed to get so far under his defences that he'd actually told her about that fishing trip with the boy Daniel.

He flipped his laptop shut, moving his eyes involuntarily to the window and through the glass, to the fractured outline of a small, wooden cabin that was just visible from where he was sitting.

His shoulders tensed. When Lottie had asked him about his family he'd told her part of the truth.

Maybe he hadn't expressed it very eloquently, but he'd wanted her to know that meeting Daniel and his family had been a transformative moment for him. Like falling down a rabbit hole into Wonderland, except in reverse, for in his family there had been no end of mad tea parties and pools of tears.

In Daniel's family cabin he'd found a bolthole from the drama, and every minute he'd spent there had only made it clearer to him that one day he would need a separate space, away from his family. He loved them, even when they exhausted and infuriated him, but he couldn't live with them.

His fingers tapped impatiently against the desktop.

But he could *live with Lottie and Sóley.*

He was already doing so, and he wanted the

situation to continue—even more now, after what had happened yesterday.

Suddenly he felt as if some invisible force was squeezing his chest. Watching his daughter take her first steps towards him, then catching her as she fell, he had felt something crack inside him as the swell of pride at her reaching the milestone of walking had battled with panic that one day he might not be there to catch her when she fell.

Three amazing, overwhelming, unrepeatable minutes of his life—Lottie's gift to him.

Only he hadn't wanted it to be his alone. He'd needed to share it with her. As he'd pulled her into his arms he'd been on the verge of asking her to stay longer, but then she'd offered to send him the video of Sóley walking, so that he could share it with his family, and something had held him back from speaking his thoughts out loud.

And it was still holding him back now.

Fear.

The word tasted sour in his mouth.

He didn't like it that fear was dictating his actions, but truthfully he was scared of what would happen if he asked her to stay on. Maybe if it had just been sex, as he'd told himself it would be, or if he simply respected her as the mother of his child it would be okay, but as he'd watched, felt, listened to her quiet devastation as she talked about her father's rejection his anger had been monumental.

Only what if, like the rest of his family, his emotions got too big to be contained?

He pushed the thought away uneasily.

They won't, he told himself firmly. He had a lifetime of experience in separating himself from his feelings—why should dealing with Lottie be any different?

His eyes snagged on the title of the topmost document in the pile on his desk. Even without the double distraction of Lottie and his daughter, he would find it perilously hard to be distracted by a report on *Strategic Pre-interaction Behaviours Using Emerging Technologies*. But it was the suggested date of a meeting to discuss the report that made his fingers stop tapping against the smooth desktop.

December twenty-first.

Sóley's birthday.

His gaze returned to the view outside his window. This time, though, his eyes were drawn upwards to the sky.

After days of pale grey silvery cloud today the sky was a limitless ice-blue, stretching out above the snow-covered fields like the ceiling of a Renaissance cathedral.

It was a perfect day.

He breathed out slowly. Maybe he had found a way to reset his goals after all. It would be a first step for him—a different kind of icebreaker from the one they'd first shared, but something he could give to Lottie.

With the determination of having finally made a decision, he pulled out his phone and punched in a number. 'Ivar. I need you to be ready in about an hour. No, just a short trip. Thanks.'

Hanging up, he glanced at the watch. Now all he needed to do was talk to Signy.

Pressing her face closer to the curved window, Lottie gazed down at snow-covered land, half-heartedly trying to imagine what it might look like in summer.

It was her second flight in a helicopter, and once again she had no idea where she was going, but this time, with Ragnar's fingers wrapped around hers, her feelings were very different. Instead of being tense with nervous apprehension, her stomach was tingling with excitement.

She watched as Ragnar leaned forward and tapped Ivar on the shoulder.

'Just over the ridge will be fine, if that works for you.'

The pilot nodded. 'Yes, sir.'

The sound of the helicopter made normal speech impossible and both men were having to raise their voices.

Dropping back into his seat, Ragnar gave her hand a quick squeeze, and then her heart picked up speed as he bent closer and she felt his warm breath on her throat.

'Just another couple of minutes.'

She felt her body soften as his mouth found hers. Her head was swimming, and she had to lift her mouth from his to stop herself from deepening the kiss and tearing at the layers of padding that separated them from one another.

'Until what?'

'Wait and see.'

Ivar landed the helicopter exactly three minutes later.

Flecks of snow whipped up by the rotor blades whirled around them as Ragnar climbed out and then lifted her down. As she pulled her hood up over her hair she looked up at him questioningly.

'So where now?'

He took her hand. 'This way.'

They crunched steadily through the snow,

up a curving bank, and then abruptly the snow ended and she felt her feet stall. She pushed her hood back from her face. In front of her a lead-grey sea stretched out to a horizon that looked as though it had been drawn with a ruler.

And next to the sea was the beach.

Only this beach was nothing like the pale, biscuit-coloured sands of home—it was black.

Lottie let Ragnar lead her down the shifting dunes.

'It's lava,' he said as she reached down and picked a handful of tiny black pebbles. 'When it reached the sea it stopped and cooled instantly. That's the dull, scientific explanation, anyway.' His mouth curved up. 'But I still can't stop myself from looking for dragons every time I come here.'

The pull of his blue gaze was intoxicating and irresistible. She smiled back at him. 'So what are we waiting for? Let's go see if we can find one.'

It was the most amazing place, Lottie thought as they made their way across the gleaming wet sands. Apart from the noise of the waves hitting the shore at regular intervals, the only other sound was the occasional seabird crying as it swooped above the water far out at sea.

'Do you like it?'

His blue eyes rested steadily on her face and she nodded, her vocal cords suddenly paralysed by the intensity of his gaze.

'Enough to stay for lunch?' he said softly.

Lunch? She frowned. 'Where are we going to eat lunch?'

And then she saw it.

At the back of the beach, where the white snow met the black stones, was a huge fire pit filled with burning logs. Around it, fat kilim-covered cushions were spread out invitingly over a collection of shaggy sheepskin rugs, and a picnic basket was sitting on top of what appeared to be a table made out of snow.

Lottie breathed out unsteadily. Something was wrong with her. A shard of ice seemed to be lodged in her throat, but her eyes felt as though they were burning.

'I don't understand…' she whispered.

He pulled her against him, brushing the tears from her cheeks. His jacket was quilted, hers was too, but she could still feel his heart beating through the layers of fabric and insulation.

'It's my way of saying thank-you for yesterday. For letting me share Sóley's first steps.'

Cupping her face with his hands, he kissed her fiercely and she kissed him back, relieved to have an outlet for the dizzying intensity of her longing for him.

Finally, they drew apart.

'How did you do all this?'

He glanced away. 'Signy and Ivar did all the hard stuff.'

She swallowed. There was a fluttering fullness in her chest she didn't understand, like happiness mixed with nerves—only she didn't feel nervous.

'But it was your idea?'

'I didn't just want to say what I was feeling, I wanted to show you,' he said.

Taking his words into herself, she leaned into him and kissed him again, until he groaned against her mouth and pulled away from her. Catching sight of the expression on his face, she smiled.

'Later,' she said softly, catching his hand. 'Come on—let's eat.'

There were soft rolls filled with sticky pulled pork or buttered lobster, and a creamy artichoke dip with crisp vegetable *crudités*. To follow there was hot mulled cider and some delicious *kleinur*—an Icelandic pastry that was like a twisted cinnamon-flavoured doughnut.

'Signy is a genius,' Lottie said when finally she

couldn't eat another mouthful. 'Are you feeling better now?'

She spoke playfully, liking the way his eyes gleamed in response to her teasing, but liking the weight of his arm around her waist more.

He pulled her closer. 'No.' His eyes locked with hers. 'But *you* feel wonderful.'

Her heart skipped forward. She felt wonderful too. Lighter, calmer. Happier. For the first time since her father's rejection she didn't have the nagging sense of being inadequate. Ragnar made her feel special and secure. He made her feel differently about herself.

A tic of uncertainty beat in time to her pulse.

But it wasn't just *her* feelings that mattered— her father had taught her that—and right now Ragnar had given her no reason to think this was anything more than just a thoughtful gesture.

'Is it always this empty here?' Glancing across the deserted beach, she frowned. 'Where I live there's always someone on the beach. Dog walkers, or teenagers having a bonfire party, or windsurfers.'

He took a moment to reply. Then, 'People don't come here because it's a private beach.'

It took a moment for his words to sink in. 'Is it *your* beach?'

He nodded. 'It came with the estate. There's a lot of protected wildlife up here, so it's probably for the best that there aren't hordes of people traipsing all over it.'

His eyes met hers, and she could see he was weighing up something in his head.

'Actually,' he said slowly, 'you're the first person I've ever brought here...and you and Sóley are the first people to stay at my house.'

She stared at him in confusion. Was that true? And if it was, why were they the first? And why was he telling her now?

His skin was taut over his cheeks, and she could feel a tension in him that hadn't been there before—a kind of rigid pose, as though he was bracing himself before jumping off a high-dive board.

Her own stomach tensed, but the question was waiting to be asked. 'Why hasn't anyone stayed at the house before?'

He stared past her. 'I didn't want anyone else before you,' he said finally. 'I come here to escape.'

Of course—he came to recharge, to rethink his business goals. Only she knew from the forced steadiness in his voice that he wasn't talking about work, and she thought back to when she'd asked him about living here.

'Was that why you went to Daniel's house when you were a child? Because it was an escape.'

His eyes were still watching the horizon. 'Pretty much.' His mouth twisted. 'It was difficult at home. My parents were arguing a lot. They got divorced shortly after that holiday.'

It seemed to Lottie that her head had never been so full of questions. She picked one at random. 'What happened then?'

'They remarried—both of them—quite a few times, actually. I have four stepfathers and three stepmothers, two full sisters and one brother, and the rest are halves and steps. It's all quite complicated and full of drama.'

He'd used that word before. 'What kind of drama?' she asked.

He shrugged. 'Oh, you know...the usual hallmarks of a good soap opera. Jealousy. Infidelity. Power. Pride.'

She stared at him in silence. His voice was calm and even, but for some reason it jarred with the mocking smile that accompanied his statement.

'But you love them?' Watching his eyes soften,

she felt the same fluttering fullness in her chest as earlier.

'Very much. But this place—' he glanced back down the beach to the dark, jutting rocks '—is dramatic enough as it is.' His gaze returned to her face. 'Does that make sense?'

She nodded.

Truthfully, she didn't fully understand what he was trying to say, but she did understand how hard it could be to try and express yourself. Just like her, words weren't his thing—but the fact that he'd opened up to her was what mattered.

'I do understand.'

His arm tightened around her. 'I was hoping you would.' He hesitated. 'And I was hoping, too, that you might consider staying on here with Sóley a little longer.'

Her heart was thumping against her ribs. 'How much longer?'

His eyes were suddenly very blue. 'I thought maybe you might consider staying here for Christmas.'

'Christmas?'

He misread the shake in her voice. 'I know it's a lot to ask, and you've probably got other plans, but I really want to spend it with—' His face tensed into a frown and he paused. 'I really want us to spend it together. The three of us… as a family.'

His admission made the breath slip down her throat . Beneath the jerkiness of her heartbeat she felt a fluttering moth's wing of hope, even though she knew it was ridiculous to wish for something she could never have.

'You don't have to make up your mind now.'

He was right. She should give it some thought, but there was no point. It was what she wanted.

'I'd like that. A lot,' she said simply.

His fingers pushed through her hair, tipping her face up to meet his lips. 'I don't know where this is going with us, but I don't want it to be over yet.'

Something stirred inside her chest, moving stealthily, swelling against her ribs so that breathing was suddenly a struggle. She pushed against it, but this time it wouldn't go away.

'I don't either,' she said.

Not yet, not ever.

Her pulse was pounding in her head. He wasn't offering her permanence. He wasn't offering her a future beyond Christmas. But that didn't seem to matter to her heart.

She had fallen in love with him anyway.

She grabbed the front of his jacket to steady

herself. Of course she was in love with him. Somewhere deep inside she knew that she'd always been in love with him—ever since that first night in London. But closer to the surface she felt panic.

She was unbearably conscious of being in love. But there was no need to tell him what she was feeling. She'd done that before—told a man what she was thinking and feeling too quickly, without filters—and she wasn't going to do it again. She couldn't risk the swift sting of rejection.

Right now what mattered was that incredibly, miraculously, he wanted her to stay.

But with Ragnar so close, and with his words echoing inside her head, the urge to blurt out her feelings was almost overwhelming.

She was desperate for the oblivion of his mouth on hers and, pulling him closer, she kissed him fiercely, losing herself in the heat of his response, letting the synchrony of their desire stifle her need to confess her love.

CHAPTER NINE

'ARE YOU COLD?'

Tilting her face, Lottie gazed up at Ragnar and shook her head. They hadn't made it into the bed—instead were lying on top of a luxurious white fur throw, her limbs overlapping with his, his arm around her waist.

'No, I'm not,' she said truthfully.

Heat was radiating from his body into hers, and the fur beneath them was incredibly warm and soft. Only...

She twisted against him, pressing closer. 'Actually, I was going ask you, just out of interest, what exactly am I lying on?'

In the heat of passion the sensation of fur against bare skin was intensely erotic, and usually she was too spent afterwards to speak, much less formulate a question. There had always been a kind of frenzied intensity to their lovemaking—maybe because they both knew that there was a time when this would end, and their imminent separation was at the back of their minds. But now they had given themselves more time they could allow themselves to savour these moments of exquisite easy intimacy.

She thought back to yesterday's conversation on the beach. It still didn't feel quite real, but it *was* real—it had happened, Ragnar had asked her to stay on with him in Iceland, and even though she knew it was just a couple more weeks, his hesitant words were making her dream of something she'd always thought life would deny her.

He shifted against her and, dragging her attention back to the present, she met his gaze—or tried to. But he was looking anywhere but at her.

'I was hoping you wouldn't ask that.' His gaze met hers.

She stared at him uncertainly. 'Why? What is it?'

He sighed. 'It's fake.'

'Oh, you.' She punched him on the arm. 'I thought you were going to say it was a polar bear, or a seal or something.'

But she wasn't angry with him. She couldn't be. Not when she could hear the smile in his voice. Shaking her head, she moved as if to roll away, but he grabbed her and, pulling her beneath him, he stretched her arms above her head, capturing her wrists with his hands.

A beat of heat ticked through her blood as he stared down at her, his blue eyes gleaming. 'I'm not a complete barbarian.'

Her body twitched as she met his gaze. They were teasing each other, using the intimacy of sex to test their relationship. 'And you're happy to say that lying naked on a fur rug?'

His lips curved upwards and she felt her heart begin to beat unsteadily. Now she couldn't just hear his smile, she could see it. Her breath caught in her throat. He might not smile much, but when he did it was as miraculous and warming as the first rays of midwinter sunlight on her face.

'I'm not lying on a fur rug,' he said softly. 'I'm lying on you.'

He shifted against her, and as the hard muscles of his chest brushed against her nipples she felt her body stir. 'Yes, you are…but I'm not sure how that disqualifies you from being a barbarian.'

Holding her gaze, he drew the tip of his tongue softly over her bottom lip, pulling at a thread somewhere deep inside her.

'What are you thinking?' he asked.

She stared at him dazedly. 'That I want you,' she said hoarsely.

His eyes narrowed, the pupils flaring, and he rolled over, taking her with him so that suddenly she was on top. Her eyes drifted hungrily over the muscular contours of his chest and she felt his hands move from her waist to her hips, his fingers biting into her skin as she pushed down against him.

He gritted his teeth and his hand caught hers. 'Give me a minute.'

His eyes were dark and glazed, and she felt his fingers tighten around hers as he fought to gain control. Glancing down, she saw that he was watching her, and his blunt expression made heat unspool inside of her. She started to move against him, wanting, needing to still the insistent ache between her thighs.

Her body was losing its bones…she could feel herself melting… Leaning forward, she clasped his face in her hands and kissed him frantically. He kissed her back deeply, licking her mouth until her body was shaking and hollowed out with desire.

'I want to feel you inside me…' she whispered.

His jaw clenched tight and, taking a breath, he rolled off her on to the fur and reached into the drawer by the bed. She watched impatiently as he rolled on a condom, and then he took her face in his hands again and kissed her fiercely, catching her hair as her searching fingers closed around him.

He sucked in a breath as she began to stroke, and then he was moving against her hand, his dark, glazed gaze watching her steadily as he reached down and lightly touched her breasts. Her nipples tightened and she moaned softly, and then his hand moved from her breast to her stomach, then lower still, his fingers tangling through the triangle of hair, teasing a path between her thighs so that she was raising her hips, seeking more of his tormenting touch.

'No...not this way—'

His fingers found hers and he freed himself from her grasp. Then he turned her gently but firmly so that she was facing away from him. Leaning into her, he reached under her stomach to caress her nipples, his fingers pulling at the swollen tips, and then he was parting her thighs, stroking the slick heat, making sure she was ready for him.

'Yes,' she whispered. 'Yes...'

Pushing back, she guided him inside her and began to move against him in time with the pulsing urgency of her heartbeat, heat spreading through her like a fever as he thrust up inside her, his body jolting into climax in time with hers...

Breathing out softly, Ragnar inched backwards, making sure that he didn't wake the woman sleeping beside him. It was early—too early to get up—but his brain was brimming with unasked and unanswered questions.

Away from the distracting warmth of her body it would be easier to think straight—or at least think instead of feel.

His phone was on silent, but he picked it up anyway, in case its vibrations or flickering screen inadvertently disturbed Lottie.

Closing the bedroom door softly behind him, he made his way quietly through the silent house, moving instinctively in the darkness. Downstairs in the living room he made his way across the rug to where the still glowing embers of the fire spread a soft red light across the walls.

Crouching down, he picked up a couple of logs and pushed them into the amber-tinged ashes. Watching the flames creep over the dry wood, he leaned back against the sofa, stretching his legs out towards the fire's reviving warmth.

It had been long time since he had woken so early, and more specifically woken with his eyes feeling so heavy in his head that it was as though he hadn't closed them at all. Nearly twenty years, in fact, since that day when he'd gone to Daniel's house and realised that he could step back from his parents' explosive marriage.

His spine tensed against the sofa cushions.

Maybe it would have been different if he'd been the second or third child, but as the firstborn there had been no diluting the impact of their relationship on him, and his parents had been fiercely in love. Every encounter for them had been an emotional collision. Even their kisses had looked like a form of fighting to him, and as a child he'd often wake early, with his head still ringing in the aftermath of yesterday's feuding.

Going downstairs, he would huddle up in front of the remnants of the fire from the night before. It had been cold and dark, but it had been the only time of the day when he could find the silence and solitude he craved.

And now he was here, in his own home, doing exactly the same thing.

His phone screen lit up and, picking it up, he glanced down automatically to check his notifications.

It was a text from his mother, and there were four missed calls from Marta. His mouth twisted into a reluctant smile. He could imagine his sister's outrage at being asked to leave a message. She wasn't used to such treatment—particularly from him—but he didn't have his phone on at night now that he was with Lottie.

The words echoed inside his head. *Now that he was with Lottie.* It was a simple sentence, but what did it mean?

He let out a long, slow breath.

He knew what it meant now and up to Christmas. It meant the three of them living as a family, eating meals together and playing in the snow, and it meant that at night he and Lottie would retreat to her room, moving inside and against each other's bodies until that dizzying mutual moment of swift, shuddering release.

But what would it mean after Christmas?

He swore softly. That was what had woken him this morning.

Out on the beach it had seemed to make perfect sense. Of course he wanted to share Sóley's first birthday and spend Christmas with her as a family, and inviting Lottie to stay on had felt like an obvious step. Now, though, he couldn't understand why it had felt like such a big deal—

or why he'd chosen to make it about his daughter's birthday instead of what it was really about.

His hand tightened around the phone.

He'd told Lottie that he would be honest with her, but how could he be when he wasn't even being honest with himself.

So be honest!

This wasn't just about playing happy families for the sake of their daughter—in fact it wasn't really about Sóley at all. He had a relationship with his daughter now, a bond that would endure beyond any fabricated deadline, and he wasn't going to let anything come between them.

But what about Lottie?

Where did she fit into his life in the long term?

Leaning forward, he picked up another log, and edged it carefully into the embers.

If he'd asked himself that question at any point up until the night in the pool house, when he'd handed her the robe, his answer would have been *nowhere*—except as Sóley's mother, of course.

He'd had casual affairs throughout his twenties, but no serious relationships, and he'd never wanted anything more—never wanted anyone for more than sex. To do so would mean getting out of his depth and too close for comfort.

But he wanted Lottie.

Maybe at the beginning their hunger had just been an urgency from which neither of them could turn away. Only now it was different.

Now, after the shortest time, she felt essential to his life—and yet he was still shying away from what that meant.

He gazed into the red core of the fire. Given what he knew about people's behaviour when they went from casual to committed, that was completely understandable. To him, relationships were unpredictable and challenging. His family had proved that time and time again. There were so many risks—so many unknowns for which there was no neat algorithm.

His mouth twisted. Or perhaps it wasn't the unknown that scared him but the acknowledgement of his own shortcomings that was making him hold back.

The fact that his parents and siblings acted as though they were living in a modern-day Asgard had never impacted on anyone but himself before now, but Lottie was unsure of her place in the world—could he really risk introducing her into the chaos of his family life?

He had no right to expect or ask that of her.

More importantly, he couldn't introduce her to

them because he hadn't actually told his family about her or Sóley yet.

His spine tensed.

Telling them was not as simple as it sounded. Not because his family would judge—they wouldn't—but because they would want to be involved, and being involved on their terms would mean being consumed. In an instant he would be fighting for control.

He would tell them soon. But on his terms. Calmly, quietly, individually. But for now he wanted to keep Lottie and Sóley to himself, for just a little longer.

Maybe that thought had been in his head when he'd asked her to spend Christmas with him. At the time, on the beach, with panic swirling up inside him like spindrift off a snow-covered mountain, he'd justified it to himself as a first small step, a baby step...

His mouth curved upwards and he felt the rise of fierce pride and happiness as he pictured his daughter moving towards him with slow, unsteady certainty. His smile faded.

Except he wasn't a baby.

He was a grown man, and he needed to start acting like one—because for the first time in his life he was more scared of losing someone than of letting them get close to him.

Rolling onto her front, Lottie lowered her face and closed her eyes. Sóley was having her nap and Ragnar was holed up in his office, reading through business proposals. She hadn't felt like sketching today. Instead, she had sneaked out to the pool house and, after a quick dip in the steaming water, she made her way to the sauna and was now stretched out on one of the slatted wooden benches.

Beneath the towel she felt warm and weightless.

Of course that was due in part to the voluptuous heat of the sauna. But it was Ragnar's invitation—and this time it *was* an invitation—to stay on in Iceland that had wiped all tension from her body.

Her heart swelled against her ribs.

It wasn't a big deal, she told herself for perhaps the tenth time since waking. It was just a couple of weeks. Only she could sense that the words hadn't come easily to him. And he hadn't had to say them at all, so surely that did make it into some kind of deal.

They would be together, properly together, so

his inviting her to stay must mean that he liked her. The thought made her pulse dart forward and she allowed herself a moment of pure, incredulous happiness.

She was growing drowsy now. And as her limbs grew heavier she felt the air currents shift and knew that someone had come into the sauna. Even without looking she knew it was Ragnar.

Opening her eyes, she looked sleepily up at him. He was wearing a towel, knotted low around his hips, and as her gaze skimmed his powerful body her sleepiness vanished instantly and her nerves started to hum like an electricity substation. Against the soft fabric the lean muscles of his chest and stomach looked like burnished bronze, and as he walked towards her she felt her insides tighten around a ball of hard, pulsing heat.

'I thought you were working.'

'I was.' Sliding onto the bench beside her, he dropped a kiss on her half-open mouth. 'I got through it quicker than expected.' His eyes slipped slowly over the bare skin of her shoulders. 'But then I had an incentive…'

She bit her lip. Her skin was prickling, and she could feel the tips of her nipples pressing into the towel. 'Incentive? Is that how you see me? As some kind of carrot on a stick?'

His long dark lashes flickered up and, blue eyes narrowing, he reached out and hooked a finger under the knotted towel above her breasts. 'That's not what I was picturing in my head, no.'

Pulling her closer, he tipped up her head and ran his tongue lightly along her lips. She moaned against his mouth, arching her body upwards, blindly seeking more contact.

'Have you got a condom?'

'No...' He groaned softly and kissed her hard, his lips parting hers, and then slowly he released her. 'I was so desperate to get down here I didn't think.'

Her stomach flipped over at the sweet look of regret on his face. It was flattering to know that she affected him so strongly, but there was a tension beneath his skin as though he was bracing himself, or building up to saying something that was on his mind.

Her heart began to thump inside her chest. 'Let's just go upstairs,' she said quickly.

'No. I don't want to go upstairs.' His voice was hoarse, but it was the tension in his arms that made her stop talking and stare at him uncertainly.

'I didn't mean that.' Gritting his teeth, he reached out and touched her cheek. 'I do. It's just there's something I want to say to you. About you and Sóley staying on for Christmas. When I asked you on the beach I made a mistake—'

In other words he'd changed his mind.

She stared at him miserably. Beneath her legs the solid bench felt suddenly as though it was made of paper. He'd had time to think and of course he'd changed his mind—but she wasn't going to let him know about the stupid hope in her heart.

'It's okay—I get it,' she said woodenly. 'You're a busy man and you've already taken three weeks off.'

'No, that's not what I meant.' His face was taut. 'I asked you to stay on here, but what I really meant to ask—what I should have asked you— was will you move in with me when we get back to England?'

She stared at him in mute disbelief, stunned by his unexpected miraculous question.

He stroked her face gently. 'I'm not good with words, and I didn't make myself clear yesterday, so I'm going to try a little harder this time. I want *you* to move in with me, Lottie. Sóley too, of course, but I'm asking *you*.'

Lottie pressed her hand against her mouth. Everything was spinning out of reach, her breath, her heartbeat, her thoughts. He wasn't saying that he loved her, but he wanted her—and not just for sex, but for herself. And right now that was enough.

'I want that too, but are you sure?'

His hands tangled in her hair and he drew her forward. 'More sure than I've ever been.'

And, tilting her face up to his, he kissed her.

Warmth flooded her body and she felt her bones start to soften. He was wrong, she thought. He was good with words—but he was even better at kissing.

For Lottie, the rest of the day passed in a kind of bubble of invulnerable happiness. At first she could hardly believe what had happened, but then Ragnar told Signy, and she'd finally allowed herself to accept that for once the hopes and expectations of her imagination had matched up with real life.

The following morning they woke early, reaching for one another in the darkness, making love slowly, taking their time. Afterwards Ragnar held her close to him, so that it felt as though his blood was pulsing through her veins.

As the sun started to ease into the room they

could hear Sóley, gabbling to herself from next door. Lottie inched away from Ragnar's warm, solid body.

'No, I'll get her,' he said.

She shook her head. 'I want to—you always get up first.' Leaning forward, she kissed him softly on the mouth. 'Why don't you grab some more sleep?'

His gaze drifted slowly over her naked body and she felt her breasts start to ache.

'I'm not actually feeling that sleepy...'

They stared at one another, a pulse of desire rebounding between them—and then there was a short, imperious shout from the other side of the wall.

His eyes locked with hers and then the corner of his mouth curved upwards. 'It's fine. I'll go and hit the gym for an hour.' Shifting against the bedding, he grimaced. 'Maybe two.'

Lottie fed Sóley her breakfast and then had a piece of toast herself. Signy had taken the morning off to visit her sister, so it would be a treat to cook breakfast for both of them. Imagine cooking breakfast being a treat. She smiled. It was just one small example of how her life had changed over the past few weeks.

The biggest and best change was that she and

Ragnar had both managed to overcome the false start they'd made twenty months ago in London. Okay, he hadn't said that he loved her, but then she hadn't said it either—and besides, she smiled, neither of them were good with words.

Picking up Sóley, she glanced down at her daughter's cereal-splattered dungarees. 'How did you get so mucky?' She sighed. 'Come on, then, let's go and clean you up.'

They were less than halfway up the stairs when she heard the sound of a car in the driveway.

It must be Signy. Except Signy would let herself in, she thought, frowning as there was a sudden frantic knocking on the door, followed almost immediately by someone pressing the doorbell insistently.

She stared at the door uncertainly.

Ragnar hadn't said anything about visitors, and the house was so off the beaten track it couldn't be anyone looking for directions. It was probably just another delivery of work papers for him.

She glanced up at the discreet security video screen in the wall and felt her spine stiffen. That didn't seem very likely. Standing in front of the camera was a young, very beautiful woman with white-blonde hair, wearing ripped jeans and some kind of shaggy astrakhan coat.

A young, beautiful, weeping woman.

Heart pounding, Lottie punched in the security code and opened the door.

'Oh, thank goodness—I thought there was no one here.'

Storming past her without a word of explanation or even a nod of acknowledgement, the young woman pulled out her phone and with tears still pouring down her face began frenetically typing.

'You can bring that in,' she called shakily over her shoulder.

Lottie watched in stunned silence as a slightly apologetic-looking taxi driver carried in an expensive, monogrammed suitcase.

'Oh, you need to pay him. You *do* understand English, right?'

Still too stunned to speak, Lottie nodded.

After paying the driver, she closed the door and turned to face the young woman. She had stopped typing into her phone, but she was still crying, and yet her smudged mascara and swollen eyes didn't detract from her quite extraordinary beauty.

Lottie stared at her in confusion. *Who was she?*

The question was barely formed in her head when the woman finally looked at her straight on and her arresting blue eyes instantly and un-equivocally provided the answer.

'You must be Marta.'

The woman frowned. 'Yes, I am.' Despite her tears she spoke disdainfully, as though her identity should be a matter of common knowledge. 'Is Ragnar here?'

Lottie nodded. 'He's in the gym.'

Marta sniffed. 'He must be in holiday mode.' Her eyes narrowed on Sóley, as though seeing her for the first time. 'I'm surprised he lets you bring your baby to work.'

'Oh, I don't work for Ragnar,' Lottie said quickly. 'I'm Lottie—Lottie Dawson. And this is Sóley.'

She hadn't been expecting to meet Ragnar's sister, so she hadn't given much thought to how Marta would react to her words, but blank-eyed bewilderment probably wouldn't have been high on her list—or on her list at all.

'Who?' Marta stared at her, her lip curling.

'Lottie...' She knew there was a slight tremor in her voice, but there was something unnerving about Marta's cool, dismissive gaze, so like her brother's and yet not. More unnerving still was the stinging realisation that Ragnar's sister had no idea who she was, or what she was to him.

The happiness and certainty of earlier fell away. She felt as though she was gripping on to a cliff-edge.

Breathing in against the feeling of vertigo filling her head, she held her daughter closer, taking comfort in the tight grip of her arms.

What should she say? Even if she had the right words, the thought of saying them out loud was just too daunting—for how could she reveal what Ragnar had so clearly decided to keep secret? Only why would he keep his daughter a secret from his sister? And was it just his sister or his whole family?

'Marta—'

Lottie turned, her heart pounding. Ragnar was walking down the stairs and clearly he'd dressed in a hurry. His hair was wet from the shower and his shirt clung to his body, where his skin was still damp.

'What are you doing here?' he said softly.

Bursting into tears, Marta bolted towards him and, watching his arms pull her close, Lottie felt suddenly like an intruder. Whatever it was she needed to ask Ragnar, right now he needed to take care of his sister.

'I'll leave you two to talk,' she said quietly and,

sidestepping Marta's sobbing back, she forced herself to walk upstairs.

For the next two hours she tried hard to distract herself from what was going on downstairs. It helped that Sóley was extra demanding, refusing to be put down for a moment and wanting her mother's full attention. Probably she'd been upset by Marta's distress, but thankfully she was too young to have understood Ragnar's deceit by omission.

Lottie shivered. A lump of ice was lodged in her stomach and she could feel its chill spreading outwards. Why hadn't he told his sister about their daughter? It didn't make any sense. He'd spoken to Marta countless times—how could he not have mentioned her?

Maybe he hadn't wanted to tell her when she was so upset. Then again, he had a big family, so maybe he was telling them one at a time.

Glancing down, she saw that Sóley had fallen asleep. Even with her blue eyes out of the equation, the family resemblance between her daughter and Marta and Ragnar was unmistakable. It was there in her jawline and the shape of her mouth.

Turning, she felt her heart stutter. Ragnar was standing in the doorway, his gaze resting on her face. He looked tired. Instantly she forgot her own fears and, walking across the room, she pulled him against her. She felt him breathe out, and the lump of ice in her stomach started to melt.

'Shall I put her down?' he asked.

She nodded and, lifting his daughter up, he laid her gently in the cot.

'Let's go downstairs,' he said quietly.

The hall was empty and silent, the kitchen too.

Lottie watched as Ragnar poured two glasses of water and handed her one.

'Is Marta okay?'

He nodded. 'She will be.'

'She probably needs some food. I can make her some lunch—'

'You don't need to do that.'

'Oh, I don't mind—'

'No,' he said firmly. 'You don't need to do that. She'd not here.'

She frowned. 'Not here. Where has she gone?'

'To Reykjavik. To a hotel.'

'But she was so upset. She shouldn't be on her own—you should go after her.'

His face stilled. 'That would be a little absurd as I was the one who sent her there.'

She stared at him, not understanding. 'You sent her away? But why?'

'This is my home. I have rules. And Marta broke those rules. She knows I don't have people to stay here.'

His answer both irritated and confused her. 'She's not "people". She's your family.'

He shrugged. 'I know—and I particularly don't have my family here. This is a place of calm and order. I don't want their drama under my roof.'

Rules. Drama. What was he talking about? She could feel panic clawing up her throat. 'But you love them.'

'Yes, I do. And I show that love to them in many different ways, twenty-four-seven. All they have to do in return is follow my rules, and the first and most important rule is that they don't turn up unannounced.'

He sounded as though he was explaining a scientific law, like gravity, not talking about his family.

'But love doesn't have rules…' she said slowly.

'Which probably explains why so many people are unhappy.'

She felt a chill as his blue gaze met hers. His eyes were hard and unreachable.

'I love my family but I can't—I *won't*—live

with them. I keep everything separate and contained. That's how it works. That's how I live.'

The hurt in her chest was spreading like a blizzard.

'Is that why you didn't tell Marta about me and Sóley?'

She saw the truth in his eyes before he even opened his mouth, and it hurt so badly she had to grit her teeth against the pain in her heart.

'Yes.'

'Have you told *anyone* in your family?'

This time he shook his head.

She breathed out unsteadily. It had happened again—just like with her father. They had met too late. Ragnar, the man she loved, the man she so badly wanted to love her, was someone who couldn't be what she wanted or give her what she needed. Only she'd been too busy painting pretty pictures in her head to see what was actually in front of her nose.

'What if I tell you that I love you?' she whispered. 'Would that change anything?'

As he shook his head the distance in his eyes made her almost black out.

'I want to go home.' The words left her mouth before she knew they were there. 'I want to go back to England—now.'

He glanced away, and there was a long, strained silence.

'Then I'll go and speak to Ivar,' he said finally. 'I'll leave you to pack.'

And without meeting her eyes he turned and walked out through the door.

CHAPTER TEN

STANDING BESIDE THE fire in the middle of the living room, Ragnar breathed out unsteadily. This was his home, and yet he felt adrift—disconnected and dazed.

He didn't know which was more unbelievable. The fact that Lottie and Sóley were gone or that he had stood and watched them leave.

He fumbled with the equation in his head but nothing he did would balance it.

He shivered. He felt cold, and the house was so quiet. No, not just quiet—it was silent. The silence of reproach and regret.

His eyes flicked across the empty room to something square and yellow, poking out from beneath a cushion on the sofa. Slowly he walked towards it, his heart pounding as he saw what it was.

Lottie's sketchbook.

He picked it up, his hand shaking as he turned the pages, an ache flowering like a black orchid inside his chest.

What had he done?

Or rather what hadn't he done?

Why hadn't he stopped her leaving?

Why had he just stood and waited while she packed?

It made no sense. He'd only just asked her to move in with him, and she'd agreed, and for the first time ever he'd been thinking about a future that offered something other than lives lived separately with clearly defined borders. For the first time ever he'd been looking at a hazy rose-gold sunset of a future, with Lottie and his daughter.

And then Marta had arrived, crashing into his ordered, tranquil life, trailing snowflakes and suitcases and disorder in her wake, and instantly the sunset had been blotted out by the need to act quickly and decisively.

Of course he'd taken care of her, but there had been no possibility of her staying. And he'd tried to explain that to Lottie. Tried to explain that he couldn't let his family into his home with all their tears and traumas.

Only she hadn't understood, and she'd kept on pushing and pushing, and then—his breathing faltered—then she'd told him she loved him.

He could still see her face now—the expression of shock and hurt when he'd more or less told that her love didn't change how he felt. He gritted his teeth. Except he hadn't said anything. He'd just shaken his head like a robot.

But he hadn't been able to make his voice work. Marta's random appearance was such an unsettling reminder of what would happen if he allowed the separate strands of his life to overlap, that her astonishing words and his own fever-ishly joyous response to them had been silenced.

Of course, seeing Lottie upset had hurt— badly—but not enough to blank his mind to the fear, so that when she'd told him she wanted to go home he'd told himself that it was for the best.

But it wasn't.

It was the biggest mistake he'd ever made.

The next few days were interminable, and he realised that time was *not* a great healer. Being alone in the house—or worse, in his bed—was like pressing against an open wound, and after one more day of agonising solitude he went down to the stables and led Camille out into the yard.

He rode blindly, seeing nothing, caring about nothing, just trying to put as much distance be-tween himself and his silent home as he could. But when they reached the top of a hill Camille slowed and, leaning back in his saddle, he gazed down at the waterfalls. His eyes blurred—and not because of the freezing wind.

The sky was dark and low and the wind was bitterly cold against his face. Any rational, sane person would be happily sprawled out on the sofa in front of a log fire. But he didn't feel rational or sane or happy. And that was why he was here, roaming the freezing hills.

It was ridiculous and illogical to act like this.

Signy certainly thought so.

Probably Camille, too, but thankfully horses couldn't talk.

Only he didn't know what else to do.

For years he'd relished coming here. Even before *ice/breakr* had gone global it had been a place of sanctuary—somewhere he could take a breath before the next storm hit.

His hands tightened against the reins.

But not any more. Now his house was an empty, echoing reminder of his stupidity and cowardice. For so many years he'd had to fight to keep his life orderly and tranquil, and now he had succeeded in achieving his ideal. After expelling Marta from his home, even his family were keeping their distance—only instead of relishing his solitude he hated it.

He missed Lottie and Sóley.

Without them life had no purpose, no value.
But she deserved a better man than him.

So be that man, he told himself. *Be the man she needs you to be. Find her and fight for her.*

And, turning away from the waterfall, he pushed Camille down the slope towards the only future he wanted—a future he was not going to let slip away again.

Looking up at the Suffolk sky, Lottie flinched as a few flakes of snow landed on her face. She was standing in the back garden of her cottage, supposedly trying to decide where to put Sóley's swing. All week it had been threatening to snow, but of course it had to wait until today, her daughter's birthday, to actually make good on its promise.

As if she didn't have enough reminders of Ragnar Stone already in her life.

All the shops were filled with fur throws and cushions for Christmas, and when Lucas had finally managed to drag her to the pub one evening she'd caught sight of a blond man crouching in front of the open fire and, ignoring her brother's exasperated protests, had simply reversed back out through the door.

But of the man himself there had been nothing.

Not a word in nearly three weeks.

No phone call.

No text.

She swallowed against the ache building in her throat.

Not even a birthday card for their daughter.

A mixture of misery and anger flared inside her. She still couldn't accept that he was acting like this—punishing Sóley for what had happened between the two of them. It seemed so small-minded and cruel, so not like Ragnar.

Or maybe it *was* like him.

Remembering the cool, almost clinical expression on his face when she'd told him she loved him, she shivered. After hearing him talk so dispassionately about his family, and his ruthless dismissal of Marta, she'd been mad to tell him that. But then she'd naively been assuming that her words would mean something to him, that they would matter—that *she* mattered.

Her mouth twisted. But they hadn't—and she didn't.

And now she was here, back in Suffolk, it was difficult to see why she had ever thought he cared about love *or* her.

Truthfully, she barely knew him—she'd just made herself feel that she did, letting the intoxicating power of their lovemaking weave a spell not just over her body but her mind too. She'd been so flattered, so desperate to believe in the story she'd told herself in her head of two people separated by circumstance but destined to be together.

She bit down on a sudden choking swell of tears. She was stupid. And selfish. For it was her fault that her daughter—her beautiful, sweet daughter—would never have a father in her life. But clearly Ragnar had meant what he said about keeping his life separate and contained.

'Lottie—'

Hearing Lucas's voice, she swiped the tears from her cheeks and took a quick, calming breath. If she could take one positive away from this whole mess it was that it had made her realise how close she and Lucas and Izzy were as a family.

Her brother and her mother were fundamentally different from her in so many ways, but she understood now that it wasn't just nature that mattered. Ragnar had taught her that nurture was just as important. Since she'd stumbled into the cottage, with tears pouring down her face, both Lucas and Izzy had been utterly amazing.

Those first few days back in England she had

felt adrift from everything—like the survivor of a sinking ship, she had only been capable of clinging to the wreckage. Then, when the shock had faded, she had been ill, stricken with cramps, immobilised by the crushing weight of failure and disappointment.

And all the time, despite everything that had happened, she'd missed Ragnar. The nights were bad, but waking was worse, for each morning she had to work through her grief and her loneliness all over again.

It was her family who got her out of bed, and dressed, and she was so lucky to have them.

Forcing her lips into a smile, she turned towards Lucas.

He sighed. 'Oh, Lottie, we agreed. No crying today.'

'I'm not crying.' She met her brother's sceptical gaze. 'Honestly. It's just the cold. I'm fine, really.'

'So, did you decide where you want it?'

She gazed at him blankly still lost in thoughts of Ragnar. 'Want what?'

He groaned. 'The swing, Lottie. Remember? I said I was going to put it by the vegetable patch and you didn't want it there—'

Without warning, she felt her face crumple. 'Sorry, I forgot.'

'No, I'm sorry.' Reaching out, he pulled her against his battered leather jacket. 'I'm just feeling cranky, but I shouldn't take it out on you.'

She pressed her face into her brother's chest, breathing in his familiar smell. 'You didn't—you've been great, Lucas.'

Looking up at him, she watched his jaw tighten.

'I want to kill him, you know. For how he's treated you and Sóley.'

'Well don't.' She smiled up at him weakly. 'We need you here—not in prison.'

His face creased into a reluctant smile. 'Is that your way of telling me you know where you want the swing?'

It took over an hour to make the frame and fix it into position but, despite the numerous setbacks, Lottie found it strangely relaxing. At least trying to make sense of the comically inadequate instructions took her mind off Ragnar, and the swing was lovely. Made of wood, it had two seats—one for a baby and one for an adult.

Lucas took hold of the frame and tried to jiggle it. 'Look at that.' He grinned at Lottie. 'Rock-solid.'

'Oh, well done, darling.' Izzy was standing

by the back door, holding Sóley in her arms. 'It looks fantastic. Shall we give it a try?'

But as she tried to put Sóley into the baby seat her bottom lip protruded and began to wobble.

'Here, let me try, Mum.' Reaching out, Lottie took her daughter.

'Look what Lucas has made. Isn't he clever?' she said softly.

She felt Sóley relax at the sound of her voice but when she tried to lower her into the seat the little girl just grabbed her neck and refused to let go.

'I'm sorry, Lucas.' Looking over at her brother's disappointed face, Lottie felt her stomach twist with guilt.

Since getting home, Sóley had stopped being the easy-going baby she had always been. She was clingy, and often woke several times in the night. It was tempting to tell herself that it was just her age, or her teeth, or even the change in routine, but she knew that Sóley was missing Ragnar as much as she was, and that only added to her feelings of guilt.

'You'll be okay, you know...' Her mother leaned forward and kissed her cheek. 'You're stronger than you think. Strong enough to survive this. And Sóley will be okay too. Children are very resilient.'

'I don't *want* her to have to be resilient,' she said hoarsely.

'I know, darling.' Izzy smiled. 'But that's nature's way. You have to be tough to survive. Look at everything I put you and Lucas through. No father figures, let alone actual fathers, and all those different homes and schools, and always having the wrong clothes.'

Her mother was looking straight into her eyes, and in that moment, the calmness of her expression made Lottie realise that she had focused too much on their differences instead of how much they were alike.

She shook her head. 'It wasn't that bad.'

Lucas caught her eye and grinned. 'It was pretty bad—especially the clothes.'

Lottie smiled. 'But whatever happened you were always there, Mum. And we were lucky to have you.' As she spoke, she wondered why she had never said that to Izzy before and why it felt true now. 'I'm lucky to have you, then and now.'

'Me too,' Lucas said, his eyes gleaming. 'Only don't go getting the wrong idea and start thinking that this love-in means you get to wear any of your weird kaftans to the party.'

Izzy and Lottie both laughed.

'Right, darling,' said Izzy. 'I'm going to take my granddaughter home with me so she can have a nap. No.' She held up her hand imperiously as Lottie started to protest and then gently pulled Sóley into her arms. 'She needs a nap and you need a little time on your own to make your peace with today. Come on, Lucas.'

After the car had driven off Lottie went and sat on the swing. It was starting to snow again, but it wasn't that cold, and it was calming just to sit and let her feet scuff against the ground. Glancing up at the sky, Lottie breathed out, trying to find the peace her mother had mentioned.

Her emotions were not out of control now. She felt sad—but not the crushing misery of those early days, just a lingering emptiness that she couldn't seem to shift. And that was okay, because her mother was right. She was strong and she was going to survive.

And because she was strong she was going to put her sadness aside this afternoon for the sake of her family—especially her daughter.

Ragnar Stone was not coming to this party so she certainly wasn't going to let the memory of him ruin it for her or anyone else.

Her body stilled. From beyond the hedge she

could hear the sound of a car making its way up the lane. No doubt her mother had forgotten something crucial, and sent Lucas to retrieve it. As she swung gently back and forth she heard the car stop in front of the cottage, and then the crunching sound of footsteps on the path. Then the click of the garden gate. Definitely Lucas, then. Her mother could never open it without a huge tussle.

'So what did you forget?' she called out. 'I'm going to go with either your phone or Mum's bag.'

'Actually, I didn't forget anything. I let it slip away.'

Her heart turned to stone. She stared across the garden, her breath dissolving in her lungs. Ragnar was standing at the edge of the path, his clear blue eyes fixed on her face. He looked just as he always had, and the pain of seeing him again made her feel lightheaded.

'What are you doing here?' Her voice sounded small and unfamiliar in the sudden echoing silence.

'I came to talk to you.'

Her throat tightened. He made it sound as though he was just dropping in, when the reality was that he hadn't been in touch for weeks. Two weeks and six days, to be precise.

She swallowed, pushing back against the ache in her chest. 'In case you've forgotten it's our daughter's birthday, so I don't really have time for a chat.'

He didn't move. 'I know it's her birthday, and I want to see her. But I have something I need to say to you first.'

'I don't want to listen to anything you have to say, Ragnar.' She stood up abruptly, letting go of the swing so that it banged into the back of her legs. 'Do you really think you can just turn up here for her birthday? It's been nearly three weeks.'

'I know. And I'm not proud of myself.'

'Well, that makes two of us.'

He sucked in a breath as though she'd slapped him. 'You have every right to be angry with me.'

Angry? *Angry?* She stared at him, the word spinning inside her head like the ball in a roulette wheel.

'You think I'm angry?' She shook her head. 'I'm not angry, Ragnar. I'm hurt.'

Crossing her arms in front of her chest, she clenched her teeth. She was not going to cry in front of him.

But as he took a step forward she felt her eyes fill with tears.

'I'm sorry,' he said softly, and the softness in his voice hurt more than anything else, for that was what she missed most. 'I'm sorry,' he said again. 'I never meant to hurt you. I would never hurt you.'

'You're hurting me now.' Her arms tightened around her ribs. 'You had no right to come here. I was just starting to feel okay.'

'I had to come. I had to come and see you.'

'And now you have—so you can go.'

He didn't move. He just stood there, with snow-flakes spinning slowly around him.

'Ragnar, please.' The hurt broke through her voice, and as she pressed her hand against her mouth he was walking towards her and pulling her close. She pushed against him. 'You have to leave.'

'Please give me a chance.'

'To do what? Throw my love back in my face?' She shook her head. 'It's too late, Ragnar. Whatever you think is going to happen here, it isn't.'

'I love you.'

'No.' She shook her head. 'You don't get to say that. That's not allowed.'

'I thought love didn't have any rules?' he said quietly.

His voice was strained, and now that he was closer she could see dark smudges under his eyes, and he looked as if he'd lost weight.

Blanking her mind to the idea that he might be suffering too, she shook her head again. 'You don't love me,' she whispered. 'And more importantly I don't love you. Not any more.'

His eyes were steady on her face.

'I don't believe you. I think you do love me, Lottie. And I know that I love you.'

Reaching out, he caught her hand, but she pulled it away.

'You think that's all it takes? Just three little words. Well, I've got three words for you. Separate and contained.'

'But I don't want to be separate from you.' He took her hand again, and this time the fire in his voice stopped her pulling away. 'I can't be separate from you. I thought I could—I thought that was what I wanted, what I needed. But I need *you*.'

'So why did you let me leave?'

Leaning forward, he pressed his face against her. 'Because I was stupid and scared.'

'Scared of what?'

She was holding her breath.

'Of feeling. Of how you made me feel.'

The shake in his voice made her eyes burn.

'My family feels everything so intensely, and when I was kid it used to scare me, being around that kind of intense emotion. And then, when I met Daniel that summer, I realised there were other ways to live. All I needed to do was take a step back, keep my distance.'

She felt him breathe out unsteadily.

'I shouldn't have let you go. It hurt so much, but I kept telling myself that I was doing it for the right reasons. That I couldn't be the man you needed and so I'd just end up hurting you.'

Remembering his tense expression when he'd found Marta in his house, she thought her heart might burst with understanding and relief. So it had been fear that had made him put his sister in a taxi. Fear, not indifference, that had stopped him from telling her what was in his heart.

'So what's changed?' she said softly.

His hands were shaking. 'I did. I realised that I didn't have a choice. I can't live without you or Sóley. I'm going crazy without you.'

He was laying his heart bare, saying the words she'd longed to hear, and yet she was scared to hope, scared to believe that they were true.

She felt his fingers tighten around hers.

'I didn't believe it could happen to me. I didn't think I could fall in love. And then it came so quickly and completely—and that scared me, because I didn't think I was capable of giving you the love you deserve.'

His eyes softened.

'My family are crazy when they're in love, and I didn't want to be like them. And then I realised that I'd been so fixated on all the ways I didn't want to be like them that I'd stopped seeing all the ways I did. Like how brave and generous and loving they are.'

'I know what you mean,' she said slowly. 'I did the same thing with my mum and Lucas, reading too much into our differences.'

He stared at her uncertainly. 'Did you mean what you said? About not loving me.'

She shook her head slowly. 'I want to mean it, but I can't.'

Sliding his arm around her waist, he kissed her. She felt him breathe out shakily against her mouth.

'I love you,' he said.

'I love you too.'

His eyes locked onto hers. 'Enough to be my wife?'

Looking down, she felt her heart swell. He was holding a ring with a sapphire as blue and clear as his eyes.

'Let me try that again,' he said hoarsely. 'Will you marry me, Lottie Dawson?'

She was nodding and smiling and crying all at the same time.

'That *is* a yes, isn't it?'

She nodded again. 'Yes, it is.'

As he slid the ring onto her finger she pulled him closer. 'So what happens next?'

He smiled. 'This...' he said softly.

And, tilting her face up to his, he lowered his mouth and kissed her.

EPILOGUE

Six months later...

GLANCING OUT OF the window, Lottie bit her lip. Why was it taking so long? Surely they must nearly be there.

But the scenery scudding beneath the helicopter's whirling rotor blades was no help at all—mainly because it looked nothing like it had the last time she'd seen it, just over six months ago. Then, it had been covered in snow, but now the snow was gone, and the land was a patchwork of colours and textures—a bit like her sixth form art project, she thought, a bubble of laughter squeezing out of her chest.

'What's so funny?'

Meeting her brother's gaze, she shook her head. 'Nothing, really. I was just thinking about an art project I did at school.'

'Okay...' He raised an eyebrow. 'You did eat breakfast, didn't you?'

'Yes, I did. I had muesli and yoghurt and fresh fruit.' She poked him gently in the ribs. 'So, what do you think?'

It was Lucas's first visit to Iceland, and she was desperate to hear his thoughts—to find out if he felt the same way as she did about this incredible country that was now like a second home to her.

'Of your breakfast?' He grinned. 'Oh, you mean of all this.' Shaking his head, he blew out a breath. 'What can I say? It's right out there… I mean, look at this place!' He leaned forward, his eyes widening as they flew over a huge vivid green field of moss. As he looked back at her, his face softened. 'I can see why you love it so much.'

She smiled. 'It's just so beautiful and rugged and remote.'

His eyes gleamed. 'Are you talking about Iceland? Or Ragnar?' he said softly.

Looking down, she stared at the sapphire ring on her finger. 'You do like him now, don't you?'

She thought back to the moment when she and Ragnar had walked into her mother's garden together, after he'd proposed. Lucas hadn't liked him at all then, but thankfully Sóley's babbling open-armed excitement at seeing her father had meant that his disapproval had been limited to a stiffness of posture and a murderous scowl.

Her pulse skipped forward. It had been a shock, seeing her normally easy-going brother like that, but it hadn't lasted. Ignoring her panicky protests, he and Ragnar had gone for a walk the next day, and when they'd returned they hadn't been brothers-in-arms, exactly, but Lucas had welcomed him as a brother-in-law.

She felt him shrug beside her.

'Yeah, he's not the worst. I mean, I wouldn't ask him to join the band, but he's pretty handy with a pool cue.' As she looked up to meet his gaze, he rolled his eyes. 'I like him, okay? He knows a lot of stuff but he's not boring about it, and he's generous with money but not flash.' His mouth twitched. 'Oh, and he's got some *extremely* hot sisters.' He hesitated, his face suddenly serious. 'But mainly I like him because I can see how much he loves you, and I know that he makes you happy.'

She swallowed against the lump in her throat. 'He does...he really does.'

Her heart contracted. Ragnar had worked so hard these last six months to turn his life around. He'd started by introducing her and Sóley to his family, and he hadn't stopped there. He'd talked to each of them in turn, explaining how he'd felt as a child and then as a man. It had been really difficult for him, but he'd been determined to deal with his fear and committed to their future—his and hers and their daughter's.

She'd been scared of meeting his family, and it had been terrifying. They were all so glamorous and emphatic. But almost immediately she'd realised that beneath all the drama there was a solid core of unbreakable love and, even though they'd been at loggerheads for months, the first time she'd met Ragnar's mother, her ex-husband Nathan, his new wife Kim and their new baby had been there too.

It had been surreal, but kind of wonderful.

A bit like his family.

The family who had welcomed her into their hearts.

Lucas frowned. 'Hey, you promised no crying.'

As Lottie swiped at her eyes she felt the helicopter start to slow. 'We're here,' she said softly.

Her heart gave a thump as they landed, and then he was sliding back the door and climbing out, holding up his hand to help her down.

'Here.' He took her hand and slid it through his arm. 'Let's go find your man.'

Her man. Her Ragnar.

Her chest squeezed tight and, gripping Lucas's arm to steady the trembling of her heart, she started to walk towards the beach, to find the man she loved without limits.

The man she was going to marry today.

'She's here.'

Glancing up, Ragnar felt the twist in his stomach muscles loosen. Behind him, his brother and best man Rob gave his shoulders a reassuring squeeze.

'Shall I get the bridesmaids?'

Ragnar glanced over to where a giggling Sóley was holding hands with his sister Marta. Their blonde hair was gleaming in the sunlight, their faces tipped back as they fled from his brother, Gunnar, across the black sand.

'No, it's okay. They're having fun.'

Turning his head, he gazed at the rest of his family. They were standing in a casual semicircle, and his eyes moved slowly from one smiling face to the next.

It was true—everyone was having fun. There had been no arguments or tears or sulking. He felt an ache around his heart. They were all trying so hard, because they loved him. And he loved them as he always had, only now it felt so much easier to love and be loved.

He felt his gaze pulled back across the sand to where Lottie was walking towards him.

And that was down to her.

Lottie had made this happen.

She had made him stronger. And kinder. She and Sóley had made loving as simple and natural for him as breathing, so that now he found it difficult to understand how he'd survived for so long living as he had.

But everything was different now—particularly him. He no longer kept those he loved most at arm's length—and, incredibly, now that they could come and go at will, his family seemed like different people too, less intense, less demanding.

More fun.

That word again.

It was so not what his life had been about before, but now he had fun every day.

A flicker of heat skimmed over his skin. He had passion too. And tenderness. But most of all he had a love that was as warm and bright and unending as the summer solstice—and that was why he'd wanted Midsummer's Day to be their wedding day.

Straightening the cuffs of his dark suit jacket, he breathed out unsteadily.

Lottie stopped in front of him, her hand trembling against her brother's arm, her face soft and serious.

He stared at her, his pulse beating in time to the waves curling onto the beach.

She looked amazing. Fitted to her waist and then spilling out in layers of tulle, her white dress was perfectly offset by the black of the sand beneath her feet. She was holding a bunch of wild flowers picked by Sóley and Marta from the fields surrounding the house, and her hair was loosely caught up at the base of her neck.

She had never looked more beautiful. And, meeting her gaze, he felt the ache in his chest intensify.

Her eyes were shining with tears of emotion, and the same emotions that were shining in his eyes were filling his heart. A happiness like no other, and a gratitude that life had let them find one another not once but three times—a statistic that had no basis in logic and was just the beautiful, disorderly, topsy-turvy mathematics of love.

'You look beautiful,' he whispered.

The celebrant stepped forward and smiled. 'Shall we begin?'

As they spoke their vows tears were sliding down his face—tears he would never have allowed to fall before meeting her.

Finally, they exchanged rings, and the celebrant smiled again. 'And now you may kiss, as husband and wife.'

They each took a step forward and then, as he lowered his mouth to hers, she leaned towards him and they kissed, softly at first, and then more deeply, to the appreciative applause of their watching families.

'I can't believe we're married,' she whispered, gazing at the gold band on her finger.

'I can't believe I made us wait so long.' Cupping her face in his hand, he brushed his mouth against hers. 'But it had to be this day.'

Her heart swelled with love as she looked up at him curiously. Ragnar had chosen the day, and at the time she'd assumed he'd picked it because Midsummer was a day of celebration for Icelanders. But the shake in his hand now told a different story.

Reaching up, she stroked his cheek. 'Tell me why you chose it?'

'It's the summer solstice.' He hesitated, struggling to contain the emotion in his voice. 'That means the sun will never set on our wedding day. I just liked the idea of that.'

'I like it too.' Tears filled her eyes and throat and, pulling him closer, she kissed him softly. 'I love you.'

'And I love you. So very much.'

For a moment neither of them could speak, but as Ragnar lowered his mouth and kissed her again Lottie knew it didn't matter. Sometimes words were irrelevant.

* * * * *

LET'S TALK
Romance

For exclusive extracts, competitions and special offers, find us online:

Want even more
ROMANCE?

Join our bookclub today!

'Mills & Boon books, the perfect way to escape for an hour or so.'

Miss W. Dyer

'Excellent service, promptly delivered and very good subscription choices.'

Miss A. Pearson

'You get fantastic special offers and the chance to get books before they hit the shops'

Mrs V. Hall

Visit millsandbook.co.uk/Bookclub
and save on brand new books.

MILLS & BOON